.

Fishers of Menace

FAITH AND FOILS
COZY MYSTERY SERIES #1

WENDY HEUVEL

OLDE CROW PUBLISHING

Fishers of Menace
Faith and Foils Cozy Mystery Series – Book 1

© 2020 by Wendy Heuvel

Published in Ontario, Canada, by Olde Crow Publishing.

Cover design by http://StunningBookCovers.com

Publisher's Note: This novel is a work of fiction. Names, characters, places, and incidents are either products of the author's imagination or used fictitiously. All characters are fictional, and any similarity to people living or dead is purely coincidental.

ISBN: 978-1-7772-1831-7 (paperback edition)
ISBN: 978-1-7772-1832-4 (hardcover edition)
ISBN: 978-1-7772-1830-0 (e-book)

Printed in Canada and/or the United States of America

Fishers of
Menace

Chapter 1

Splash.

A piece of muffin fell into Cassie Bridgestone's tea.

"Argh!" Cassie fished out the soggy chunk with a spoon and wiped the crumbs off the café table.

Her best friend, Lexy, and sister-in-law, Maggie, stifled their snickers.

"What's with you this morning?" Maggie twisted her cup on its saucer.

"She's nervous about the new tenant." Lexy giggled. "She's hoping he's tall, dark, and handsome."

Cassie frowned. "You know that's not it. I woke up jittery. Not sure why." She wiped more crumbs from her lap. "Besides, the tenant is an old retired guy. He's not even good-looking."

"I thought you hadn't met him yet." Maggie furrowed her brow and popped a piece of doughnut into her mouth.

"I haven't." Cassie smirked. "But that doesn't mean I haven't researched his online profiles."

The girls laughed.

"So, you're admitting you checked him out? I knew it was time to find you a date!" Lexy winked.

"You both know I'm not ready. Besides, I did no such thing." Cassie sat up straight in her chair. "You don't think I'm going to rent a store and an apartment to just anyone, do you? I check out all the applicants."

"Did any of the other applicants offer you a year's rent up front?" Maggie grinned.

"Without even seeing the place?" Lexy added.

"That might have helped with my decision." Cassie relaxed her shoulders again, and they all shared another giggle. Even though it was brief, she loved this weekly tea time, and the quaint Tea Garden was the perfect place to meet.

Cute, frilly curtains and flowery paintings adorned the windows and walls, and a delightful display of fresh pastries and chocolates called out from behind the glass counter, begging to be eaten. On their table, an antique teapot and dainty teacups surrounded a bouquet of colourful flowers in a porcelain vase.

"What about your vacation rentals? Any manly prospects for this weekend?" Lexy asked, a hopeful gleam in her eye.

"Only if your type is big, smelly fishermen." Cassie gulped her last sip of crumby tea. "It's the bass tournament weekend, remember?"

"That could be my type."

Maggie almost spit out her tea.

"What? Not all of them are big and smelly."

"That's right!" A petite woman with a black bob approached the table. "My Zachy happens to be medium-sized and smelly."

"See?" Lexy laughed.

"Good one, Anna." Cassie greeted her friend with a wave. "Want to join us?"

"I can't. Just picking up takeout." She grabbed a cardboard tray with three cups from the counter. "I'm heading to the bait shop to help the boys." Bubba's Bait Shop was one of the sponsors for the fishing tournament, and Anna dated Bubba's son, Zach.

"I'm sure they'll have their hands full over the next few days." Cassie smiled. "Maybe next time?"

"Sounds like a plan." Anna waved. "We're still on for tomorrow though, right?"

"Of course." Cassie nodded.

"What's tomorrow?" Maggie asked.

"Anna and I are going birdwatching."

"And that's why we don't get together more often." Lexy put her cup down and flipped her dark hair over her shoulder. "You prefer birds over excellent company."

"Maybe?" Cassie laughed as she fished some change out of her wallet and tossed it on the table.

Anna giggled and headed toward the door. "Have a great day, you three!"

The girls waved, and Lexy checked her phone. "Ugh. Yup. It's time to go, ladies. Work beckons."

Maggie picked up her purse and glanced at Cassie. "I've

got a couple hours of work at the office, and then I'll be in for my shift." She referred to the real estate office where Cassie's brother, Rick, was an agent. Maggie often helped her husband with paperwork since it wasn't his strength, but her main job was working in Cassie's shop, Olde Crow Primitives.

"Sounds good. See you then!" Cassie exchanged hugs with Lexy and Maggie and stepped out of the café into the sunshine.

It was going to be another beautiful day in the village of Banford and a great weekend for the fishing tournament. She lifted her long purse strap over her head and pulled at the curly hair that got snagged in the process. As she walked down Main, she admired her little town. She wished she hadn't wasted seven years living in the city. On the other hand, maybe it made her appreciate Banford even more.

Across the street, the owner of the Candle Barn swept her shop's front step. Next door, a waitress at Java Junction wiped a few of the outdoor tables, and people streamed in and out of Drummond's Bakery, letting the scent of freshly baked cinnamon rolls waft out into the street. Cassie smiled as she approached her building on the corner of Main and First. Across the way, a boat engine roared to life as it exited the lock station and headed upriver.

She turned the corner at her building. Mr. Daniel Sawyer was to meet her at eight thirty at the entrance to the store he'd leased from her. She was grateful to finally have someone take over the empty space. It'd been vacant for about six months, and although the rent from the apartments and vacation rentals upstairs covered the vacancy, it would be nice to have the space occupied again. Especially since he was turning it into a used bookstore.

A bookstore would nicely compliment her Olde Crow Primitives store and The Chocolate Shoppe in the same old, stone building. And it would be another great fit for the small, cozy town.

Cassie examined the storefront as she passed her shop. She had changed the window displays last week to a summer theme and had included some cute rustic items and wooden fishing décor, as a lot of the tournament participants brought their wives for the weekend. Banford was known for its cute stores and was a big draw for ladies on a day out.

Poking her hand into her purse, she grabbed her keys as she rounded the corner of the building. As she looked up, she let out a small gasp.

A ruggedly handsome man leaned against a black SUV. He was smartly dressed and wore expensive shoes—definitely not one of the fishermen invading the town for the weekend. What was he was doing there?

He smiled at her as she approached the door with her key extended. Cassie felt heat rise to her cheeks and focussed her attention on the lock.

She heard him step behind her.

"Are you Cassie?" His voice was deep and soothing.

She whirled around in surprise. He removed his sunglasses and stared at her with intense, blue eyes. It took her a second to find words.

"Ah, yes. Can I help you?"

"I'm Daniel."

The keys fell from her grasp and jingled as they landed on the stoop. He bent to pick them up, and as he handed them to her, she realized her mouth was slightly agape. She swallowed.

"Daniel Sawyer." He offered his hand for her to shake. "Your new tenant?"

She accepted the handshake, her hand a clammy mess. She dropped the keys again. Why was she being such an idiot?

Daniel laughed as he picked them up a second time. "Slippery hands today?"

"Yeah, I guess." She took the keys from him and fumbled with the lock again until the latch clicked.

"We were to meet at eight thirty, right?" Daniel ran his hand through his hair. "I didn't mess up the time?"

"No. Yes. I mean, yes. Eight thirty." She pushed the door open and stepped into the shop. "Sorry, I... I expected someone... older."

Daniel smiled. Cassie's stomach flipped. She wished it wouldn't have.

"Let me guess—you searched online and found a picture of my father?"

Cassie felt the heat in her cheeks again. She turned away and flipped the light switches on. "You caught me." No sense trying to hide it.

"You won't find me online as Daniel Sawyer." He turned around to get a good look at the room. "Wow! This is a great space! It's way better than the pictures portrayed!"

The store was long and narrow, running the entire width of the back of the building. Large windows with wooden grilles and deep windowsills lined two walls, and a stone fireplace stood at the far side.

"This is perfect!" Daniel walked farther into the room, causing the floor to creak as he stepped on the old, wooden planks.

Cassie grimaced. "Sorry. There's nothing I can do about the squeaks."

"No, it's fine. It adds character."

The muscles in his neck bulged slightly as he admired the high, tin ceiling. He turned to her again and locked his gaze on hers.

Butterflies fluttered around in her stomach, but Cassie quelled them by quickly looking away and heading toward the door on the back wall. "I'll show you to your apartment now."

They stepped through the doorway and ended up in the building's stairwell. "My shop is through there." Cassie pointed down another hall. "And so is an entrance to The Chocolate Shoppe. You can access the parking lot through that door there." She pointed to a big exterior door.

She started up the stairs, aware her neck burned as he followed closely behind.

"This is a nice building. Do you own the whole thing?"

"Yes. I acquired it from my grandmother." Why was she explaining that to him?

"I see. How long ago did she pass?"

Cassie chuckled. "She's still alive; she just wanted to

retire. She lives in the manor at the edge of town. We co-own the building, until I pay her off."

"Oh! That sounds like a good business deal."

"It is." Why was she still telling him her personal information? They emerged on the second floor. "A nice lady name Betty lives there." Cassie pointed to a door marked 2B. "And that's my apartment, 2A, if you need anything."

"Good to know." He smiled.

Cassie's face grew hot again. She quickly stepped into a small room. "Through here is the laundry room." She opened a cabinet. "You can store your laundry soap, and whatever, here. There's no fee for the washers or dryers, but I ask that you keep them clean and make sure clothes don't get left in them. And…" Cassie frowned.

"What is it?"

"My laundry baskets are missing."

"So, don't borrow the laundry baskets…" Daniel chuckled.

Cassie grinned as they left the room and ascended the next staircase. "Up here on the third floor is your apartment. There are two other apartments on this floor I rent out short-term to vacationers. Like this week—for the fishing tournament."

They reached the top, and Cassie was surprised she felt a bit out of breath. The stairs had never bothered her before. She made sure to hold the keys tightly this time as she unlocked Daniel's apartment door.

"Fishing tournament? Is that why it's so busy in town

on a Tuesday morning? I chose to move to Banford because it was supposed to be a sleepy town." Daniel followed her into the apartment.

"It is. Trust me." Cassie handed Daniel the set of keys. "But the tournament is a big draw. First prize is thirty thousand dollars, a boat, and a trailer. People come from all over the province to participate."

"Wow! That's a pretty big prize for a small town."

"Yes. Three local businesses work together to sponsor it—the bait shop, the marina, and the car dealership. They also get part of the money as a grant from the tourism committee."

Daniel nodded his head in approval. "Smart."

"The tournament starts Thursday and runs until Sunday. But lots of fishermen like to arrive early and scout the waters for a couple days first. The guys staying in the vacation apartments up here have already arrived." She nodded toward the hallway.

"But it's a sleepy town the rest of the year, right?"

"Yes, though tourism does keep the town hopping in the summer—and during the Christmas Festival."

Daniel laughed. "Maybe I should've stayed in Toronto!"

"It's never as busy as that." His gaze rested upon her again, so Cassie turned to avoid it. "I'd show you around the apartment, but there's not much to show. It's small, like I mentioned in our emails. Kitchen, living room, bathroom, and bedroom." She whirled around and pointed to each place as she spoke.

"It's perfect." Daniel's eyes were still only on her, not

the apartment.

Cassie's thoughts said to think he was a bit creepy—except he wasn't. Not in the least. He seemed sincere, and kind. "Well, I'll leave you to it." Cassie headed to the door. "I have to go open my shop. If you need anything, let me know."

"Thank you, Cassie." His smile made her stupid stomach flip again. "The movers should be here soon with my things. I'll be busy with them for most of the day. But maybe I'll pop into your store later and check it out."

"Sounds good." Again, with the warm cheeks. Ugh! She gave a quick smile, bolted out the door, and quickly descended the stairs to her apartment.

"Meow!" A big, round, orange-and-white tabby greeted her.

"Hi, Pumpkin! We'll go down in a minute!" Cassie cooed. Her cat was her steadfast companion and came to work with her every day.

But first, Cassie wanted to check something. She hurried to her office and rummaged through the papers on the top of her desk. When she found the stack she was looking for, she flipped the pages until she saw Daniel's lease.

It was right there on the application. His birthdate. He was only a couple of years older than her own twenty-eight years. How did she not see that before? She stared at the roughly copied black-and-white photo of his driver's licence. Now that she knew he wasn't an old guy, she could see it in the blurred photo—if she squinted. She made a mental note to accept only full-colour scans as identification from now on.

She recalled he said you wouldn't find him online as Daniel Sawyer. She checked the name on the lease again. No other name or variation was listed.

Something didn't make sense, but she couldn't put her finger on it. At any rate, she'd have to think about it later. Tossing the stack of papers back onto her desk, she rushed out the door with Pumpkin at her heels. It was time to open her shop.

Chapter 2

The next morning, Cassie tied her runners and hung her binoculars around her neck. She checked the time on her phone to see it wasn't quite seven, then shoved it into her shorts pocket, kissed Pumpkin on the head, and bolted out the door and down the stairs, into the morning sunshine.

Outside, Cassie hurried down the street at a brisk pace, the river to her left as she headed to Bubba's Bait Shop. She took a deep breath of the fresh, cool air.

The tournament would begin the next day, and boats bobbed in the water as fishermen tested for the best spots. She smiled at the familiar sound of a line being cast into the water.

Birds fluttered in the trees and bushes beside the sidewalk, singing sweet melodies to her. "Good morning, Lord." Cassie warmed as she thought of God. Although she wasn't a morning person, she enjoyed the time once she was up and moving around. Especially if it involved a walk by the river.

Anna would be waiting for her at the bait shop. Bubba was letting the girls use one of his fishing boats.

With the influx of people into Banford this week, they wanted to check on the group of Henslow's sparrows nesting downriver in a weedy field. The Henslow's sparrows were an endangered species, and this was the first time in years they'd been found breeding in Ontario. There would only be time for a quick check on the birds before Cassie had to open her store, but she didn't want to miss this opportunity.

They couldn't do much to help the birds, but she felt an obligation to check on them, regardless. The Banford Bird Club, which Cassie and Anna were both a part of, had decided not to publicize the fact that the sparrows were nesting there. They knew it would bring birders from all over the province, hoping to catch a glimpse of the rare species so they could add it to their life lists. They decided to make sure the birds had successfully hatched and fledged before they officially announced and documented their presence.

Cassie's mood suddenly shifted as an image of Daniel popped into her mind. He never did visit her in the shop the day before. Not that she wanted him to. Or did she? No. She was definitely not interested in him. He was a good-looking man, but he was her tenant and that was what he would remain. Besides, she didn't want a man in her life right now.

All the same, Cassie decided she would check in on him later. When he'd said the day before that the movers would be coming, she hadn't expected to see three trucks lining the street around the side of her building. From her store, she could hear people going up and down the stairs and banging in the bookstore all day long. She'd wanted to check in on him then, but she didn't want to give Daniel the wrong idea. He might think she was interested in him or checking on why he hadn't come into her store.

A chickadee flew in front of Cassie and landed on a nearby branch, bringing her mind to the present. She turned onto the walk to Bubba's.

Cassie tucked her hair behind her ear and pushed open the door to the bait shop. The bells on the door jangled. A number of people already browsed inside.

"Hey, Cassie!" Bubba waved.

She headed to the counter. "Hi, Bubba. Busy place this morning!"

Bubba grinned from ear to ear. "Yup. Can't beat the business during the tournament."

Cassie noticed two burly fishermen in hip waders and plaid shirts examining a wall of fishing lures. She recognized them as two of her vacation apartment renters. "Hi, Mitch. Hi, Jake." She waved as the men turned.

"Oh hello, Cassie." Mitch nodded, while Jake waved and smiled.

"Is the apartment okay? Did you sleep all right?"

"It's great, thank you." Jake gave a thumbs-up. "We didn't wake you this morning, did we?"

"No, no. I was up early of my own accord." She took a few steps toward them. "A day out scouting the waters before the tournament tomorrow?"

"Absolutely," Mitch answered. "We'll spend time fishing on the Rideau any chance we can get! The lakes and rivers are built up way too much where we're from."

An old man pushed past Cassie on the way to the cash register with an old minnow bucket in hand. "So why come up here and clutter our river then?" He scowled.

"Play nice, Lloyd." Bubba eyed the man over a display of fishing lures on the counter.

Lloyd scoffed as he put the bucket on the counter. "Fill it with a dozen baitfish, and I'll take a carton of leeches."

"Hey," a bald man in another aisle piped up. "I thought there was no live bait allowed in this tournament!"

"Calm your panties." Lloyd sneered. "I'm not in the stupid tournament. I fish for pleasure, not for money."

The bald man narrowed his eyes but returned to looking at the display of rods in front of him. "Not that you'd be much competition, anyway," he muttered under his breath, but still loud enough for all to hear.

"What's that?" Lloyd asked.

"Let it go, Lloyd." Bubba dipped his net in the bait tank to capture a few more little fish and dumped them in the bucket.

"It doesn't matter anyway," another man joined in. "I'm catching the biggest bass this year." He stood tall and pushed his glasses up his nose.

Bubba laughed. "Sure you are, Eric."

Eric smirked and approached the counter with a fishing net.

"Actually, the tournament is ours. No question." Mitch stuck his chest out and beamed.

"Shut up," Jake whispered and elbowed Mitch in the side.

Cassie grinned as Mitch's puffed chest and ego deflated at the same time.

"All right, all right." Bubba hit the buttons on the cash register and handed the bucket to Lloyd. "That'll be $20.85, please."

Lloyd pulled a twenty and a loonie from his dirty coat pocket and slammed them onto the counter. "Robbery. That's what this is."

"You could always catch your own bait instead of buying Bubba's," Eric teased.

"And you could always go home and leave the river in peace like it should be!" Lloyd retorted.

Eric raised his hand and was about to say something else when a woman stepped up beside him, put her hand on her hip, and stared him down. Eric lowered his hand.

Bubba smirked. "You tell him, Marjorie."

Lloyd dropped the change in his pocket and muttered as he shuffled to the door. "Miserable tournament. People should stay at home."

He pulled the door open and stepped out, letting it almost slam on Anna as she proceeded to walk in. "Morning, Cassie, Bubba." She waved. "Ready to go?" Binoculars swung from her neck, though they appeared too heavy to hang around her short, small frame.

"Most definitely." Cassie gave Anna a quick hug.

"Good luck today, guys." She waved at Jake and Mitch.

"Be safe. The river is busy this morning." Bubba waved as they stepped through the back and a door marked Employees Only.

"Phew. I'm glad you showed up." Cassie blew out a breath. "It started to get dicey in there."

"Men and their fishing." Anna rolled her eyes and followed Cassie down the steps to a dock behind the shop.

"And women!" Cassie added, thinking of Marjorie.

"Let's hope no one interferes with the sparrows." Anna stepped into a small fishing boat. Cassie stepped in after her, almost losing her footing as the boat rocked.

Anna laughed. "Careful there, sailor!"

Cassie shot her a joking frown and sat. "My safety depends on the captain."

"Then you better say those prayers you like to say!" Anna laughed as she pulled the cord to start the motor.

The boat lunged forward before Cassie could grab onto something. She felt herself being jerked backward but caught herself before she fell right off the seat. "Easy there, Andretti," she shouted over the noise of the motor.

"He raced cars, not boats." Anna winked. She evened out the throttle and headed upriver to the nesting site.

Cassie tilted her head up and enjoyed the wind flowing through her hair. She spotted an osprey with a fish in its talons and pointed it out to Anna, who gave her a thumbs-up in return. The male osprey was on his way to bring his female partner breakfast, as she sat on the eggs in their nest. The osprey let out a screech loud enough to be heard over the boat motor, announcing his arrival as he glided to the nesting platform. Barely visible above the edge of the massive nest of twigs, the female eagerly took the fish.

A white movement on the island ahead caught Cassie's eye. A great egret!

Anna must have spotted it, too, because she let off the throttle. The boat slowed until it came to a stop. She pointed to the island, but Cassie already had her binoculars to her eyes, scoping out the white shape.

"What's it doing out this way?" Anna asked.

"It must be from the colony farther upriver." Her eyes lit up. "Maybe they'll start a new nesting colony closer to us next year!"

Anna focussed her binoculars on the bird. "It's so beautiful."

The two girls stared at the bird for a few minutes, enjoying its white plumes as they danced in the breeze.

"And look!" Cassie pointed to the shore. "There's a green heron in that tree!"

Anna shifted her binoculars to the direction Cassie pointed.

"How did you ever see him?" Anna asked. "I can barely see it with my binoculars!"

"It's easy. You can tell by the shape of his body and the way he's sitting. And no other bird around here with the same shape would have the dark colouring like that."

Anna shook her head. "I wouldn't even have spotted it in the first place."

Cassie grinned. "Years of birding experience."

"Eagle eye, more like it." Anna put her binoculars down and started the boat again.

"Or heron eye?" Cassie grinned at her own joke.

Anna rolled her eyes and shook her head. A few moments later, she slowed the boat. This time, they were midriver. A creek headed off the shore on one side, and a grassy field was on the other. She approached the field at a slow pace, until she cut the engine altogether.

Anna grabbed the oars and dipped them into the water. She quietly and slowly rowed them a bit closer to the grassy field.

"I think we might already be too late in the day." Cassie sat ready, binoculars in hand. Henslow's sparrows woke even earlier than most birds.

"Oh, I hope not!" Anna sighed. "Why do they have to be so quiet during the day? There's probably more of the silly things all over Ontario, but no one can ever find them or get up early enough to hear them!"

Cassie laughed. "You might be right."

They approached the shore, trying to find the balance between being close enough for a good look yet far enough away not to disturb the birds. The grasses swayed in the small breeze. Bullfrogs and spring peepers sang loudly from the swampy creek across the river.

"What's that?" Cassie pointed. A reed of grass moved differently than the rest. She expertly focussed her binoculars on the spot and briefly caught a glimpse of the cute yellowish-brown bird. "There! Did you see it?"

"No," Anna sighed. "Of course not."

Cassie pulled out her phone to glance at the time. "We have a bit longer before I have to open the store. Let's sit and wait awhile."

"Thanks! I hope that—"

A loud hum filled the air as a boat came speeding up the river. The engine roared louder as it quickly approached them.

"He's going way too fast!" Anna yelled, over the sound of the motor.

Cassie waved her arms, trying to catch the driver's attention. Nesting site aside, the boat sped much too quickly for being this close to the shore—and to their little boat.

"Slow down!" Cassie yelled.

But it was no use. There was no way her shout would be heard above the roar of the engine.

The boat zoomed past, and a hand waved back at her.

Eric and Marjorie.

Cassie braced herself as the wake threatened to capsize them. Anna rowed to turn into the waves and lessen the blow, but it wasn't enough to eliminate all of the impact.

Cassie and Anna gasped as the chilly water surged over the side of the boat and soaked them. They grasped the sides, preparing to be thrown overboard, but the boat held its own and rocked mightily without tipping.

Anna held up her soaking wet binoculars. "Oh no!"

Cassie frowned and examined her own wet Nikons.

"Argh! What were they thinking?" Anna looked upriver, but Eric and Marjorie were long gone.

Chapter 3

Cassie adjusted the towel wrapped around her body and walked into the kitchen, scrunching her curls with her hand. She hadn't intended to take a second shower that morning before opening her Olde Crow Primitives shop, but the alternative was smelling like the fishy river all day. She still couldn't believe Eric and Marjorie had almost capsized her and Anna's boat.

She put on the kettle and went to get dressed while waiting for it to boil. Since she liked to stay open a little later on Thursday and Friday evenings, she didn't open the shop until ten both days. If she hurried, she would have enough time to check in on Daniel first and maybe chat for a few minutes.

Cassie tried on a blue shirt, covered it with a navy blazer, and examined herself in the mirror. She quickly changed into a green blouse instead and then swapped it for a loose, flowery, brown tank top before the kettle whistled.

Why was she so indecisive about her outfit? She never

had that problem.

Pumpkin meowed by her dish while Cassie hurried to make her tea and poured it into a ceramic travel mug. "Nice try, fluffy butt," she chided. "I already fed you this morning." She bent to give Pumpkin a scratch on the head. "Let's go!"

The cat eagerly followed Cassie to the door and meowed when her owner stopped by the foyer mirror to put on some lipstick. "Yeah, yeah. I'm coming."

Cassie checked her phone. Nine thirty.

She looked up the stairs and then down. Would Daniel still be in his apartment? Or would he already be in the bookstore? Pumpkin ran up the stairs, so she figured she'd try the apartment first but then stopped halfway up the staircase. What if he was sleeping? She certainly didn't want to wake him. What if he slept in only his boxers? Or in nothing?

Cassie felt heat rise to her cheeks. Downstairs it was. She turned around and started her descent when one of the upstairs doors opened behind her. She looked back.

It was Daniel. And her cheeks were still flushed.

"Good morning. Looking for me?" He wore fitted jeans and a tight, white T-shirt. His bicep bulged as he ran his hand through his hair.

Cassie lost her voice and stopped halfway down a step. What was wrong with her? She needed to pull it together. She swallowed. "Hi. I, uh, wanted to check and make sure everything was all right."

"Thanks." His smile beamed as he headed down the

staircase toward her. "I'm great."

"I meant with the apartment and the store."

"Oh, of course. Yes. Everything is great. Do you want to see what I've done so far in the store?"

"Sure."

Pumpkin bounded past them.

"Ah!" Daniel jumped. "What is that?"

Cassie giggled. "Daniel, meet Pumpkin. Pumpkin, this is our new neighbour, Daniel."

As if on cue, Pumpkin stopped on the landing, turned around, and meowed.

"She's, um, rather… large."

Cassie gasped, feigning insult. "She's fluffy."

"Is that what they call it nowadays?" Daniel winked at her as he passed by the cat.

Cassie giggled. Again. That was twice in about a minute. She shook her head slightly and continued down the last flight, taking a long sip from her travel mug.

Pumpkin bounced after them and followed Daniel right to the door of his bookstore. He peered at the orange-and-white bundle of fur as he turned the key.

"She likes you." Cassie took a sip of her tea. "I can put her in my store while—"

"No, it's fine." He eyed the cat, warily. "But if she coughs up a furball, I want a deduction in my rent." He grinned and pushed the door open.

Cassie gasped. The store was lined with wooden, antique bookshelves. They'd been arranged to make little nooks along the walls. Some of them already held a few books. Other books sat in the piles of crates scattered across the floor. At the far end of the shop, inviting, cozy chairs surrounded the fireplace. A braided rug gave the space a warm feel. The whole place had been transformed in just one day.

"This is beautiful!"

"Thanks! The rest of the books arrive today."

Cassie ran her fingers along one of the wooden shelves. "These are lovely. Where did you possibly find this many matching antique shelves? They must have cost a fortune— I mean, uh..." She tried to think of something to say quickly, to overcome her blunder. How could she have said that?

Daniel didn't seem to notice. "They did, but they were worth it. I acquired them from an old library in the city."

An antique bar counter stood in the front corner of the store, with a computer and a cash register sitting on it. "And this! It's wonderful." She approached it and ran her hands across the streaked wood.

"I'm quite happy with it." Daniel followed Cassie as she walked to the seating area.

She grabbed a remote from the top of the fireplace and pressed a button. The gas flames sprang to life. Pumpkin jumped onto a chair and licked her front paw.

Cassie sipped her tea. "This is such a perfect fit for this town. I think you'll do quite well."

Daniel pointed to Pumpkin, who purred quite loudly. "If everyone is as comfortable here as she is, I might even turn a profit."

Cassie laughed. "I can't believe you've done so much already!" She strode over to the nearest shelf and browsed a few of the titles.

"The movers did most of it. I decided I wasn't going to break my back trying to lift these huge shelves."

"Oh!" Cassie squealed in delight as she knelt beside an open crate. "Mystery books!"

"Ah, a mystery buff, are you?" He leaned against the end of the bookshelf, watching her look over the books and smiling as she touched each spine.

"I love them." She pulled out an Agatha Christie novel and set her tea on the floor so she could use both hands to skim the book. "I don't think I've read this one!"

"Take it."

She returned the book to the crate and stood. "I couldn't do that. I'll come and buy it from you later."

"Don't be silly." Daniel took a step closer to her. He smelled like leather and the fresh outdoors. He reached in front of her to grab the book out of the crate. His forearm flexed as he lifted the book.

Cassie held her breath.

He held it out to her. "Seriously. It's yours."

"Well, thanks, I guess." She grabbed the book, picked up her tea, and took a step back. "But I don't see how you're going to make money if you're already giving books away to your first customer." She caught herself tilting her head in a flirtatious manner, so she quickly straightened it.

"I hope you're more than just a customer."

What did he mean by that? Cassie quickly walked to the

next bookshelf nook. "You know what you're missing here?"

"What?"

"A coffee bar." She stepped out to the center of the store, whirled around, and then pointed to the window in the middle of the long outside wall. "Right on that sill, there. If people have a cup of tea or coffee to sip on while looking at books, they'll stay in the store longer and be more likely to buy."

"Wow, beauty and brains too."

"Oh, stop." Cassie waved her hand at him but smiled. "I'm serious."

"So am I." He looked at her with that intense gaze of his, and she found herself staring into his eyes for what seemed like eternity. He finally spoke to break the moment. "I think it's a great idea. You're spot on."

"But don't tell the café owners in this town it was my idea."

He laughed. "Don't worry. It'll be our secret." He closed the gap between them until he stood directly in front of her.

Cassie stared at the carpet, scrubbing at a dot with the toe of her shoe. "So, if you need anything else…"

"I know where to find you."

"C'mon, Pumpkin!"

At the sound of her name, Pumpkin jumped off the chair and followed her owner to the door of the shop.

"A cat that listens!" Daniel grinned. "Will wonders never cease?"

Cassie grinned. "Who knows? Maybe one day I'll find a man who listens too."

She stepped over the threshold, pulled the door shut behind her, and rolled her eyes. What a dumb thing to say. She wasn't looking for a relationship. Why would she even make a joke about it? The last thing she needed was for Daniel to think she was looking for someone in her life.

The keys jangled as Cassie unlocked the door to her shop. Pumpkin leaped into the store ahead of her as an image of Daniel's muscular arms flashed through her mind. She shook her head to make it disappear and smiled like a silly schoolgirl, despite herself.

Chapter 4

"These displays are beautiful! You've done such a wonderful job." Dorothy Merrick wandered through the Olde Crow Primitives store, boasting about Cassie's handiwork to any of the customers who might overhear.

"Thanks, Grams!" Cassie felt like she'd received a warm hug. "I try hard to keep it as amazing as when you owned it." She avoided telling Grams how hard she'd worked all day the day before to keep her mind off Daniel and his biceps. Besides, the tournament opened that morning, and she'd wanted to make the shop extra nice for the wives coming into town.

"You've far exceeded what I ever did, here. You're going to have to change the name to 'The Young Crow.'"

"You neither were, nor are, an old crow, Grams!" Cassie pulled some pip berry garlands out of a box, put price tags on them, and grinned at the spunky woman and her spiky, grey hairstyle.

Grams walked up to her and gave her a tight side

squeeze. "You do me proud. You know that, right?"

Cassie returned the hug. "I love you!"

"How is the new tenant?" Grams went to the linen wardrobe and thumbed through the braided place mats and runners.

"He's fine, I guess." Cassie busied herself with hanging the garlands on hooks and avoided her grandmother's gaze. She smiled at a customer who squeezed by her.

"Mm-hmm." Grams adjusted a few wooden sheep on a shelf. "I saw him yesterday, directing the movers outside."

"That's nice." Cassie kept hanging garlands.

"He's a very handsome man."

Cassie still avoided looking at Grams. "I'm not interested."

"The colour of your cheeks would suggest otherwise."

Cassie grabbed the empty box and set it behind the cash register. "I won't deny his good looks, but I have no interest in a relationship."

Grams gently placed her hand on Cassie's arm. "Remember what the Bible says about being unequally yoked. It's important. You have to stay strong, Cassie. Don't be swayed and end up on the wrong road again."

Cassie slumped her shoulders and finally faced Grams. "I know. That's why I'm trying to keep my distance. Besides, I'm not ready for another relationship."

"Honey, it's been four years. You've got to let go and learn to trust again. You can't go through your life being lonely. Just pick the right man. Remember—he has to love God more than you, and—"

"Me more than himself. I know. But I'm not lonely. I have Pumpkin. And you!" Cassie kissed Grams on the cheek.

"Ha! That's good in theory, but I know your heart wants more. You can't keep things from me, even if you succeed in keeping them from yourself."

Cassie stared at the floor and sighed. She admired Grams's wisdom but hated when it applied to her own life.

A customer approached the cash counter with an old black lantern and two scented candles. Cassie's phone rang at the same time.

"I'll get the customer." Grams squeezed around a stack of boxes to get behind the counter.

Cassie looked at the phone screen. Anna. She usually only texted. Had something happened to the birds?

"Anna?"

Anna snivelled on the other end of the line. "Cass? Something horrible has happened."

"Oh no! Were the birds disturbed?"

"No, it's way worse!" She let out a sob.

"Breathe. Tell me what happened."

"Zach and I were fishing for the tournament, and... oh, Cassie!"

"What is it?"

"We found... Lloyd Hutchins."

Cassie struggled to make sense of Anna's words. "What do you mean? Was he missing?"

"No." Anna sniffed. "We found his body."

Cassie gasped. "What?"

"He drowned."

"Oh, honey!"

"It was horrible." Anna sniffed again.

"I bet it was awful. Are you okay? Where are you now?"

"We're at Bubba's shop."

"I'll see what I can do to get there."

Anna only sobbed in reply, so Cassie hung up and rushed to the cash counter. Grams handed the customer the paper bag with her lantern and candles and wished the lady a good day. Her smile faded when she turned to Cassie.

"What's wrong?"

"Lloyd Hutchins drowned," she whispered, out of earshot of the customers.

Grams gasped. "Oh dear!"

"And Anna and Zach found him."

Grams nodded in understanding. "You go. I'll tend the shop as long as you need."

"Are you sure? You don't mind? Maggie's shift starts in about an hour."

"It's no problem at all." Grams grasped Cassie's hand and patted the back of it. "You go be with your friend. Take as much time as you need."

"Thanks, Grams!" Cassie kissed her on the cheek and grabbed her purse from behind the counter. Pumpkin let out a little meow from her basket, perched on one of the shelves underneath. Cassie gave her cat a quick kiss on the top of the head. "Don't worry, Pumpky. Grams will look after you for a bit." She waved to Grams and bolted out the front door.

Cassie hurried down the street, alternating between a brisk walk and a slight jog. No time to admire the river and the birds this time. Anna needed her. She'd sounded so desperate and afraid on the phone. Cassie had never heard her like that before.

A siren filled the air, followed by a police cruiser speeding by. It stopped ahead, at Bubba's, where a crowd already surrounded the shop and milled about on the street. News travelled fast in Banford. Cassie darted her way between people, searching for Anna. She found her leaning against a wooden rail beside the shop, hunched over, head in her hands. Zach had his arm around her, but apparently it wasn't enough to comfort her.

"Anna!" Cassie called.

"You came." She looked up. "What about the shop?"

"Grams is looking after it." She reached Anna and gave her a big hug. "What happened?"

"It's so awful!" Tears streamed down Anna's face. "We were fishing out in the creek across from the Henslow's sparrows. There was a boat half under water by the shore. And then there was Lloyd in the weeds. Just... floating there."

"It's shallow there, so I jumped out of the boat," Zach continued. "But it was already too late."

Cassie's mind whirled as she worked through the scenario. "But we saw him only yesterday. Not to be crude, but a dead body doesn't float until after a few days."

"He had a life jacket on," Zach said.

"A life jacket? And he drowned in shallow water?"

"His leg—" Anna sobbed again. "It was tangled in the weeds."

"His fishing line was tangled too. He must have been trying to unhook it." Zach stared at the ground and kicked a pebble with his shoe.

"Zach Brooks?" A police officer called.

Zach raised his hand, and the officer waved him over.

Cassie suddenly realized how many cops were already at the shop. A second cruiser must have pulled in while she talked to Anna, and an Ontario Provincial Police boat was tied at the public boat ramp beside Bubba's. Her stomach lurched when she noticed the tarped mound on the dock. It had to be Lloyd Hutchins's body.

Zach stood on the dock, chatting with the officer, who wrote things down in a little notepad. After a few seconds, Zach lifted his hand and pointed at Anna. Then he flailed his arms around, wildly.

Cassie wondered what he could possibly be saying. "It'll be okay." She put a comforting arm around Anna. "You've had quite a shock. You'll feel better after a while."

Anna nodded as another siren pierced the air. An ambulance pulled up, and people moved out of the way as it backed into the boat dock area.

Zach jogged up the short hill, his face paler than it had been a few minutes before.

"What's wrong?" Cassie asked, as she continued to hold her arm around a now-shivering Anna.

"You're not going to believe this." Zach grabbed Anna's hand. "They're saying they believe Lloyd was murdered."

Anna gasped and threw her free hand over her mouth.

"What? You're kidding!" Cassie opened her eyes wide.

"I wish I was." He turned to Anna. "They need us to go to the police station with them and answer a few more questions."

Anna sniffled but nodded. They exchanged a wary glance.

"What station?" Cassie asked. "The big county one?"

Zach shook his head. "No, the small office here in town."

Cassie turned to Anna. "Perfect. If they're using the satellite office, then Lexy will have to unlock the door and run the front desk. You won't be alone there."

Anna nodded again. "Okay."

The officer whistled and waved his arms at Zach and Anna.

"Don't worry. It's routine." Cassie hoped that was true.

Zach put his arm around Anna and led her to the police cruiser.

Cassie pulled out her phone and texted Lexy. She worked as an office administrator in the municipal building, which housed the satellite police office. It was only open one afternoon a week, and Lexy's job included being the front office person for the policeman on duty. She also had to open the office and be present if there was any criminal activity during off hours—which was almost never. She'd be making up for it now, Cassie thought.

Lexy replied that she'd take care of Anna as best as she

could and keep Cassie up-to-date.

"Cassie!" a plump woman in her sixties called from the crowd.

Cassie turned to see Ida Brooks waving at her. Ida was Bubba's mother and Zach's grandmother. She was also a dear friend. Cassie had grown quite close to her over the years, being in the same Bible study group.

"Hi, Ida." Cassie gave the woman a warm hug.

"Isn't this horrendous?" Ida's cheek twitched. "Poor Zachy. And Anna? Sweet thing. She'll have nightmares for weeks! And, of course, there's the Hutchins family to think of and pray for." She put her hand on her hip and shook her head.

"We'll pray for them tonight. You're coming right?" Thursday night was their regular Bible study group night.

"Definitely. I wouldn't miss it. Maybe this whole situation will knock some sense into the two of them. And Bubba too. They've avoided God long enough!"

"Yes, that would be nice." Cassie sighed. Her friendship with Anna would go so much deeper if they shared the same faith. Like what she had with Lexy and Maggie.

A paramedic slammed the rear ambulance door and hopped into the passenger seat. The lights swirled and the siren let out a short whoop before the ambulance proceeded forward as the crowd dispersed.

"Poor Lloyd." Ida sighed. "He died as miserably as he lived."

A second police boat pulled up to the dock. Over the roar of the engine, the driver shouted instructions to the cop in the first boat. Within moments, both boats pulled away from the dock and sped upriver.

Cassie stayed by Ida's side as she mingled with the crowd, discussing the horrific occurrence with other townsfolk. People shared in the shock and retold the story over and over as other people arrived. As a small village, they would mourn together.

"All right! Clear the area, please!" A lady police officer in the lot stretched her arms out to direct the crowd away.

"I'd better go check on Bubba." Ida turned toward the bait shop. "Come with me?"

Cassie nodded. It was as crowded in the shop as it was on the sidewalk. The smell of fish permeated the air. The two women made their way through to the rear employee door Cassie and Anna had used the day before to access Zach's boat.

Unlike most tournaments, Bubba liked to keep the results of the weigh-ins secret until the final reveal on Sunday evening. People could still speculate on the winner, but for the most part, the suspense drove the fishermen to fierce competition. Hoping—but not knowing—that their fish had made the cut, they'd snatch up the best lures they could from Bubba's shop, get back on the river, and try to reel in something even bigger.

Behind the shop, Bubba had a tank where he kept the largest fish until the tournament was over. The rest were released live. As Cassie stepped down to the dock, Bubba pulled another fish off the scale hook and dropped it into the tank.

"I brought Cassie with me." Ida gently placed a hand on Cassie's arm.

Cassie wrinkled her nose at the fishy stench emanating from Bubba.

"Hi, Cassie."

"Hey, Bubba. How are you doing?"

"Okay, I guess." He rubbed the back of his neck. "You know whose fish that was?"

Cassie shook her head.

"Zach's. He caught it this morning before he found Lloyd. It's by far the biggest one yet."

"Bittersweet." Ida frowned.

"I'd like to be excited for him," Bubba continued. "But this whole thing is a mess."

"The crowd is breaking up now." Cassie looked into the tank at the big bass swimming around. "Things should return to normal soon."

"I hope so." Bubba washed his hand in the fish tank and shook the water off to dry it. "This weekend is stressful enough without one of my favourite customers drowning. Poor Lloyd."

Cassie gave Bubba a compassionate smile. Lloyd was a complaining old goat who disrupted customers in Bubba's shop, yet Bubba clearly still respected the man and considered him one of his favourites.

And then she realized Bubba must not know the police were treating this as a potential murder. She decided not to tell him. If it were true, he'd find out soon enough.

Bubba's phone rang. He wiped his hand on his dirty

overalls before answering. "Anna? What's wrong?"

Cassie could hear some of Anna's sobs through the phone, although she couldn't hear the words in between.

The colour drained from Bubba's face. He stumbled a step backward before sitting on the edge of the fish tank. "I'll close the shop and be right there." He hung up and looked helplessly at Ida and Cassie.

"What's wrong, son?" Ida put her hand on Bubba's shoulder.

His mouth dropped open, but nothing came out.

"Bubba?"

"That was Anna."

"And?" Cassie pressed.

"They're charging Zach with the murder of Lloyd Hutchins."

Chapter 5

Cassie fluffed a throw cushion and propped it up on the couch for a second time. A pile of birding magazines sat on the coffee table. She straightened them and tossed them in the woven basket next to her armchair. Her apartment was always spotless and didn't need straightening, but she needed to keep busy before the Bible study group arrived. Normally, she would've grabbed the latest mystery novel she'd been reading, but she didn't think she'd be able to concentrate. It had been a taxing day.

All afternoon, as tourists browsed Cassie's shop, they'd whispered about the young man who murdered someone on the river. Cassie knew there was no point in trying to correct them, but it was awful hard to stand by and listen to complete strangers talk so horribly about Zach.

When she wasn't thinking of Zach and Anna, Cassie's mind wandered to Daniel. She'd resisted the urge to pop back into the bookstore and chat. What she was really looking for was comfort, and she'd learned long ago she should only look to God for that.

She plopped down into her armchair. Pumpkin jumped from her favourite spot on the nearby bookshelf and landed on Cassie's lap.

"Oof!"

"Meow?"

"Yes, yes. I'll pet you for a few minutes."

Pumpkin closed her eyes and purred while Cassie stroked her.

She had about half an hour before people would start showing up. Ida was usually first to arrive, but after the arrest of her grandson, Zach, Cassie wasn't sure she'd be punctual.

Lexy and Maggie had both confirmed they were coming, and the pastor's wife, Fran, had said she would be there on time. Eleanor, a sweet older lady from the outskirts, was out of town that week. That was unfortunate, because she was the prayer warrior in the group.

Through texts and calls, it had been decided they would forego their regular book study on the topic of faithfulness. Instead, they would spend the evening in prayer for Zach, Anna, and their family.

Cassie knew it was the best thing they could do, but for some reason she always felt a bit embarrassed praying in front of people. It didn't make sense, because she knew prayers were always answered, but she was self-conscious, nonetheless.

Even so, she would put the feeling aside for the evening. Zach and Anna needed their prayers.

A knock on the door made Cassie jolt in her seat. Pumpkin dug her claws in to hang on.

"Ouch!" Cassie unhooked the claws from her shorts and put Pumpkin on the floor. The cat ran away, kicking her legs up behind her with a frantic burst of energy.

Cassie opened the door to find Daniel, holding a box of pizza. The smell of pepperoni and cheese wafted by, and her stomach rumbled in response. With everything going on, she had forgotten to eat supper.

"Hi." Daniel's smile lit up his face. "I, uh, grabbed a pizza, and it's too much for one person. Banford's version of a small is slightly larger than what you'd get in the city. I wondered if you wanted to share?"

"That would be great." Cassie stepped back and waved her hand to invite him in. "I didn't eat much today."

"I thought that might be the case." Daniel handed Cassie the pizza and removed his shoes. "Busy at the shop?"

"Yes, very." Cassie set the pizza on the counter and grabbed two plates from the cupboard. "And the whole murder thing, you know."

Daniel stood and straightened his T-shirt. She tried to ignore his muscles. "I heard about it. Anyone you know?"

"Sort of." Cassie sat on a bar stool, and Daniel propped himself onto the one next to her. He smelled like old books and coffee. Cassie swallowed. How could she notice that at a time like this? "I know the man, but not closely. The suspect, however, is my friend Anna's fiancé."

"Oh no. I'm sorry. I didn't realize."

Cassie opened the box and pulled on a slice of pizza,

41

stretching it until the gooey cheese gave way. She set it on a plate, passed it to Daniel, and grabbed another slice for herself.

"He didn't do it. That much is certain."

Daniel nodded.

"But the tourists through my shop today… ugh! We might as well have a public hanging in the square tonight."

Daniel let his pizza sit and propped his hand under his chin, resting his elbow on the counter. He focussed all his attention on Cassie. "I'm sorry. That must have been difficult."

Cassie buried her face in her hands. "I feel so bad for Zach and Anna! They're so young… and sweet."

She felt a gentle touch on her leg and peeked through her fingers to see Daniel's strong hand resting carefully above her knee. Her stomach fluttered, and her pulse began to race. She pulled away and quickly stood.

"I'm sorry—I never offered you anything to drink." She walked to the fridge and opened the door. "Milk, water, or iced tea?"

"Just water please." Daniel took a bite of his pizza.

Cassie grabbed two bottles of water from the fridge and brought them back to the counter as Pumpkin did a mad dash from the bedroom, around the kitchen, and out to the living room. "I forgot to mention, my friends are going to show up soon."

"Oh? Having a little get-together?"

"Something like that." Cassie gulped. Should she tell him it was a Bible study? How would he react? But she shouldn't hide it, and maybe he was a Christian too. "It's my Bible study group." She forced the words out quickly before she changed her mind. "We always meet here on Thursday nights. Tonight we're going to pray for Zach and Anna."

Daniel stopped chewing his pizza and stared at her.

"I, uh," Cassie stammered. What had she done? "Sorry. That's probably a bit weird to you."

"No, no." Daniel swallowed his food. "It's, um, endearing."

"Endearing?" Not the reaction she'd hoped for.

"What I mean is… enchanting."

"I'm not sure that's any better." Cassie furrowed her brow. She'd really blown it now. He thought she was a complete whacko.

"No one in the city—or at least the groups of people I knew—would do something like that." He spun the lid off his water bottle and then tightened it again. "It's one of the things I looked for when choosing a place to live."

Cassie suddenly felt hopeful. Was he a Christian? Or was he seeking God?

"I like the whole small-town feel," Daniel continued. "The warm and friendly neighbours, seeing familiar faces on the streets—living in a place where friendships and family are strong and the ties between them cause them to look out for one another, like you're doing tonight."

"Oh." Not quite what she thought he was going to say. "So, you're not a believer, then?"

"A believer? In what?"

And that was the clearest answer she could get. But to

humour him, she answered, "In God."

"God? Sure. I believe there's a God. I usually go to church on Easter and Christmas."

Cassie forced a smile and got up again. "Another piece?" she asked. He shook his head, so she shut the box, a gesture to symbolize the fact that the door to anything beyond a friendship with Daniel was also now shut.

Not that she wanted anything anyway, she reminded herself.

He sipped his water and screwed the lid on again. "You haven't touched your pizza." He pointed at her plate.

"Maybe I wasn't so hungry after all. But thank you for bringing it. It was thoughtful."

Daniel smiled. "Keep it in the fridge. You might want it later." He hopped off the stool and went to put his shoes on.

"I will. Thank you."

After his shoes were tied, he stood tall and grabbed for her hand. "Thanks for being so hospitable."

"You're welcome." Cassie's hand tingled. She pulled out of his grasp and opened the door as an excuse for letting go. "Have a good night."

Daniel's eyes sparkled as he smiled at her again. "You too."

Cassie shut the door, leaned against it, and sighed. Why did he make her feel so warm and electrified? This wouldn't do. He wasn't a Christian. There was no way she could pursue anything, and it was for the best.

She was just fine with Pumpkin, her friends, and Grams.

Running the store was fulfilling, and her church was amazing. And she'd remind herself every day, if she needed to.

Daniel was right about one thing. Banford was a perfect place to live, except for the odd murder.

Chapter 6

"Hi!" Lexy stepped into the apartment and gave Cassie a hug. "Who was that hot set of muscles I passed in the stairwell?"

Cassie avoided Lexy's gaze. "Daniel, the bookshop owner."

"What?" Her eyes widened. "When you told me he was actually a young guy, you failed to mention his gorgeousness."

Cassie shrugged. "No big deal."

"Tell that to your red face." Lexy smirked.

"It's not important. How were things at the station today?"

Lexy kicked her sandals off and pulled a pack of chocolate cookies out of her huge purse. "Crazy. In more ways than one." She plopped into the armchair and tossed the cookies on the coffee table in front of her. "Officer Welby is certainly a challenge to work for. I'm glad it's usually only once a week.""He must be furious he had to come in an extra day."

Lexy nodded. "Yup. And no amount of doughnuts could soothe him."

Cassie giggled, but she quickly sobered. "What's going on with the charges against Zach?"

"It's not looking good. I'll tell you all about it when everyone else gets here."

They were interrupted by a knock. Maggie walked in and set a plate of date squares on the counter. "Hi, honeys!"

"Hey, Maggie!" both girls chimed as they all exchanged hugs.

As usual, Maggie's stylish shag cut had every hair in place, and her capris and tank top were accented with a chiffon scarf wrapped around her neck. Cassie adored her sister-in-law. Her brother, Rick, couldn't have chosen a better wife. Maggie wasn't originally from the area, but it didn't take her long to fit in after marrying Rick. She was a blessing to the community, to the church, and to Cassie. She felt like a true sister, not just an in-law.

"Before I forget," Maggie addressed Cassie. "Lily has a piano recital next week and insisted I invite Aunt Cassie."

"Aw! I'll be there!" Cassie beamed. "What about Olivia? When is hers?"

"Not until next month. The older kids have a longer course."

Lily and Olivia were Cassie's adorable nieces. At ages seven and ten respectively, they were at the cutest stages in life. Everything they said or did was funny and wonderful. They were the two sweetest girls in the world—but Cassie may have been a smidge biased.

Another knock at the door announced Ida's arrival, followed shortly by Fran, the pastor's wife. Fran was both pleasant and no-nonsense at the same time, and her bobbed haircut and straitlaced clothing reflected her personality. She successfully balanced her roles as a mom, a wife, a pastor's wife, and a women's ministry leader. Cassie admired her and looked up to her, even though she was only ten years older than Cassie.

Within twenty minutes, everyone had exchanged hugs, grabbed their hot beverage of choice from Cassie's extensive pod collection next to the coffee machine, and seated themselves in the comfy chairs around the living room. The coffee table held an array of cookies, date squares, veggies and dip, and chocolate.

Pumpkin emerged from her hiding spot and made the rounds, brushing up against everyone's legs. They all petted her as she walked by.

"Fill us in, Lexy." Cassie grabbed a box of tissue and set it in the middle of the coffee table. She had a feeling they'd all need it before the night was over.

Lexy sighed. "Just remember, this all stays in this room. Some of what I tell you I'm not really allowed to share. I could get in trouble, but I want to help Zach and Anna."

They all nodded in agreement.

"They're charging Zach based on a few things." She pulled her legs onto the chair and crossed them in front of her. "First, he was wet, so it showed he was in the water with Lloyd. And his prints were all over Lloyd's boat."

"Obviously," Fran spat out. "He found the body!"

Lexy nodded. "Yes, but there's more." She sighed. "Zach has a criminal record."

"What?" Ida gasped. "What did he do? When?"

"Remember, you're not supposed to know this yet, Ida." Lexy reached forward to grab a piece of chocolate. "At least not until it shows up in the newspapers."

Ida nodded in understanding. "I won't tell. Please continue."

"Zach has two assaults on his record."

"Those?" Ida scoffed. "I know about those. They weren't even his fault! The first one he merely fought back when some drunk guy came at him in a parking lot in the city."

"And the other?" Maggie asked.

"Some idiot was yelling at a girl in a restaurant and threw a drink on her. Zach took it upon himself to be a bouncer and removed the guy from the premises. I can't believe he was charged for it."

"The fact is, he was." Lexy put a throw cushion behind her back. "And it doesn't matter if he had good intentions at the time. That's not how Canadian law works. An assault is an assault, and you can be charged, even if you were defending yourself or someone else. According to the report, he used more force than was reasonably necessary."

Cassie shook her head. "Even so, Anna was there when Zach found Lloyd. Surely her eyewitness testimony counts for something?"

"This is where it gets worse. She was nervous during the

interviews, and Officer Welby took it to mean she lied to cover for Zach. He's investigating her as a possible accessory."

"Of course he is." Cassie rolled her eyes.

"He's the cop who comes here every week?" Fran asked.

Lexy nodded. "And he hates it. He's complained to me on more than one occasion. He thinks he's a city big shot, and I think he feels it's beneath him to have to come to Banford." Lexy slid the plate with chocolates an inch closer to her and helped herself to another one.

Fran caught on. "So, it would be convenient for him if the murder investigation wrapped up quickly."

Lexy nodded, and wiped a piece of caramel from her lip.

"That's all fine and dandy, but what about a motive? How does he explain that?" asked Cassie, rising from her seat to grab her own chocolate morsel.

"The fish Zach caught was really big." Lexy stretched her hands out and held them a couple of feet apart. "Bigger than last year's winner."

"It was." Cassie nodded. "I saw it."

"And?" Ida shrugged. "So what?"

"Oh." Cassie let out a breath. "Let me guess. They're saying he took the fish from Lloyd. Lloyd put up a fight, and Zach knocked him into the water. Is that about right?"

"Close, yes." Lexy nodded. "The bruises on Lloyd neck indicate someone held him underwater until he drowned."

Fran gasped. "How awful!"

"My poor Zachy!" Ida sniffled again.

"I'm so sorry, Ida." Lexy grabbed her hand. "If I could help, I would. But with all this incriminating evidence, it doesn't look very good."

"Isn't it just circumstantial? It's not hard evidence, is it?" Cassie asked.

"True. And it will all come out in the trial, but it usually takes six months to a year before a homicide case gets to court. In the meantime—"

"He's stuck in jail!" Ida full-out cried.

Fran left her seat and went to comfort Ida. "We're going to have to pray. It's all we can do!"

"No." Cassie shook her head. The others looked at her, with incredulous stares. "I mean, of course, we'll pray, but there is something else we can do."

"What?" asked Maggie.

"We can find the real killer.

Chapter 7

Cassie stepped into the dimly lit entryway of the police office and took a deep breath, trying to muster up courage. She squeezed her purse strap as she stepped forward. Lexy waved at her from behind the reception counter.

"Hi! Any news yet this morning?" Cassie asked.

Lexy frowned and shook her head. "Nothing. Officer Welby waltzed in here an hour late and closed himself in his office. You haven't opened the store yet?"

"Grams is covering for me for a couple of hours."

"You might have to hire her!"

"Wouldn't that be interesting?" Cassie giggled.

"Miss Alexander," a gruff voice called from behind the closed office door.

Lexy rolled her eyes, hopped from her chair, and opened the door.

The tall, lanky officer stood beside his desk. He held papers in each hand.

"Yes, sir?"

"Which one of these is correct? And why are there two?"

"They're the same report, sir. I made an extra copy for the file."

Cassie held back a snicker.

He thrust one of the reports at her. "Well, don't do that. I have enough paperwork to deal with." He waved his hand to encourage her to leave his office.

"Sorry, sir, but there's someone here to see you."

"Who? Do they have an appointment?"

"A concerned citizen. I told her you were free."

Officer Welby narrowed his eyes and opened his mouth, but before he could give Lexy a verbal thrashing, Cassie stepped behind the counter directly into his eyeline.

The corner of his mouth raised into something of a grimace, not a smile. He tossed the other report on his desk and held out his hand as he sat. "Have a seat, Ms…"

"Bridgestone. Cassie Bridgestone." Cassie took the seat offered to her and noticed Lexy exited the room but left the door ajar.

"How can I help?" He picked up a pen and wrote something on a typed document.

"I'm here about the murder of Lloyd Hutchins."

Officer Welby continued writing, not even making eye contact with her. "Yes. Go on."

Cassie swallowed and wiped her palm on her pantleg. "You see, um, I happen to know Zach and Anna very well, and I think there's more to the story than what's been revealed so far."

He leaned back in his chair, folded his arms, and smirked. "Fortunately, Ms. Bridgestone, our justice system is based on facts, not on feelings. The evidence will speak for itself."

"I'm sure it will. I'm only concerned there is more evidence yet to be presented."

"What do you mean?"

"I know Zach didn't do it." Cassie tried to maintain a steady voice, despite the anger welling up within her. "Therefore, there must be more evidence, because something has to point to the real killer."

"Were you there? With Zach and Anna?"

"No, but—"

"Then you don't know he didn't do it."

Cassie straightened her shoulders. "Were *you* there? How do you know he did?"

He pressed his lips together into a thin smile and thrust out his chest. He stared her down without saying a word.

Ugh! She bit her tongue. Why wouldn't he listen? "Please. Would you consider looking into it further? I've known Zach a long time, and he would never do something like that."

"There's no need to waste manpower on an open-and-shut case." Officer Welby leaned forward and picked up his pen again. "However, if you're interested in being a character witness, you could contact his defence attorney once one is assigned. But frankly, I doubt it will do much good." He went back to writing on his document.

"I understand, but I think—"

"Good day, Ms. Bridgestone."

Cassie could feel her cheeks flush as she stood. "Except it's not a good day, is it? Not for Zach, or Anna, or Bubba's family! You're not even willing to give him the benefit of the doubt."

Officer Welby slammed his pen down and glared at her. "*That* is not my job. That's the jury's job. I collect the evidence and document the facts. All of which, may I remind you, point directly to Zach being the murderer. That is why he was charged and brought to the county station for holding."

Cassie shifted her weight from one foot to the other, desperately searching for something else to say that could possibly change his mind.

He stood and pointed to the door. "You can go now. I have paperwork to finish so I can get out of this godforsaken town."

Cassie stepped to the door but then turned back to Officer Welby. "I assure you, God has not forsaken this town. And he will not forsake Zach, either." She ignored Officer Welby's chortle as she exited the room and shut the office door behind her.

Lexy's lips formed a narrow line as she gave Cassie a quick hug. "You tried, and your efforts were better than mine."

Cassie shook her head and put her purse onto the counter with a thump. "I really thought this would go better." She sighed.

"What did you expect? You know what he's like."

"I know, but after all the prayers last night…" Cassie stared at the floor. "I guess I figured he'd be more cooperative. Or at least listen."

"We'll just have to solve the case without his help." Lexy let the copy of the report slip from her fingers and cascade through the air until it landed on the floor. "Oops! Where did that report go? I can't seem to find it."

Cassie quickly caught on, grabbed the report, and shoved it in her purse. "Thanks, Lex."

Lexy winked at her friend and gave her another quick hug. "What's your next stop?"

"I think I'll pick up some doughnuts and bring them to Mrs. Hutchins and offer my condolences on the passing of her husband."

"Good place to start. Don't forget to talk to her son too. I think his name is Judd."

"Judd?"

"Yeah." Lexy held her arms out to her sides and flexed her muscles in a hulk pose. "Big, burly guy. Bald, with a goatee."

"Sounds pleasant." Cassie frowned.

Lexy snickered. "Just your type!"

"I have a type, do I?" Cassie ignored the picture of Daniel briefly flashing through her mind.

"You definitely have a type. I, on the other hand, am much more open to different personalities and looks."

Cassie smirked. "Well, beggars can't be choosers."

Cassie received a playful swat on the arm from Lexy before she grabbed her purse and scooted out the door.

Chapter 8

After a quick stop at Drummond's Bakery, Cassie hopped into her mid-sized SUV and set a fresh box of doughnuts on the passenger seat. They immediately filled the enclosed space with the tempting smell of cinnamon and chocolate, and she pushed them farther out of her reach. She cracked open a window rather than using the air conditioning system she'd recently had repaired, hoping the tempting scent would dissipate.

She pulled the police report out of her purse and studied it. The time of death was put at between seven and eight in the morning. Other than that, it didn't hold any marvelous revelations or even any tidbits of information to help her with the case.

It did, however, have Lloyd Hutchins's address. She punched it into the GPS. The map appeared on-screen, leading to a destination just outside of the village, on the north side of the river.

Cassie steered the SUV out of the little parking lot

behind her building and waited at the only stoplight while a small pleasure yacht headed through the swing bridge and lock system. Once it passed, the swing bridge turned back into place, and the light turned green, giving her permission to pass.

As she crossed the river, she admired the swallows fiercely diving through the air, skimming the water's surface for their lunch. She only hoped she could catch the killer as swiftly as they caught their bugs.

Cassie turned right and drove out of the village. Within minutes, the GPS sang in a British accent that she had arrived at her destination. A long driveway snaked through the trees. She followed it until she came to an old, two-storey home in desperate need of paint. The gardens overflowed with weeds. Menacing vines climbed over old motors and boat parts sitting in random spots in the yard.

Cassie grabbed the doughnuts and carefully made her way to the front door. As she knocked, the window panes rattled to the point she thought they might break.

"Who is it?" a raspy voice called from inside. Cassie couldn't tell if a man or a woman asked the question.

"It's Cassie Bridgestone." No one replied, so Cassie continued. "I'm here to see Mrs. Hutchins. I brought some doughnuts."

Heavy footfalls approached, and the door flew open, catching Cassie by surprise. A husky man stood before her. "My mother's not feeling well. I'll take the doughnuts and give them to her."

Cassie ignored his outstretched hand. "You must be

Judd. I'm so sorry for your loss. I'd really like to tell your mother in person."

Judd's eyes narrowed as he studied her, but when she refused to release the doughnuts, he relented. "I'll get her."

He didn't hold the door or motion for her to come in, but Cassie took the initiative and followed him inside. One look at the dirty, uneven floor was all she needed to decide she would keep her shoes on, even though it was considered rude not to remove them. She skirted her way around piles of stacked newspapers, fishing gear, and cases of empty beer bottles, while following Judd toward the sound of a television game show. Cassie wrinkled her nose at the pungent odor of cigarette smoke and sweat. She gulped to try and reduce the shock of the smell.

A grey-haired woman was rocking in a 70s print La-Z-Boy and looked up at Cassie when she walked in. Her hair was pulled up into a bun, and wire-framed glasses sat on her nose.

"Ma?" Judd pointed at Cassie.

"Who are you?" She squinted through the glasses.

"Hi, Mrs. Hutchins. My name is Cassie Bridgestone. I own the Olde Crow Primitives store in town."

"Oh." She turned back to the television.

"I wanted to drop by and offer my condolences for the loss of your husband." She held the box out toward Mrs. Hutchins, who merely pointed at a cluttered coffee table, directing Cassie to place them there.

Judd took the box from her hand and helped himself to a maple doughnut. He put it in his mouth to hold it and, with his free hand, grabbed a powdered one too. He handed the box back to Cassie and sat on a tattered loveseat.

Cassie placed the doughnuts on top of a stack of magazines and gingerly sat on the edge of an afghan-covered couch. Mrs. Hutchins continued to watch the television, but she grabbed the remote and turned the volume down.

Taking that as a good sign, Cassie tried to initiate more of a conversation. "I'm so sorry for your loss. It must be a tremendous burden for you both."

Judd nodded, half of a doughnut still hanging out of his mouth.

"Serves him right, going in those weeds." Mrs. Hutchins squeezed her lips into a thin line. "I've told him a thousand times he was too old to be climbing out of that boat."

"He did that often?"

She nodded. "Always said the best fish hid between the shore and the boat. The only way to catch 'em was to get out in the water with them."

"It worked, didn't it? He caught a huge fish." A piece of doughnut fell out of Judd's mouth as he spoke and landed on the floor.

"One that got him killed!" Mrs. Hutchins scowled. "Silly old fool. He probably tried to fight that boy off instead of just handing him the fish willy-nilly."

Cassie fought to keep her expression neutral. As much as she wanted to defend Zach, this wasn't the time or place to declare his innocence. Especially if she wanted to get any information. "Was there anyone else who may have wanted to hurt your husband?"

"You mean besides my ma?" Judd slapped his knee and guffawed.

"Hush, boy! Ain't no time for joking."

Judd shoved the last half of the powdered doughnut into his mouth. The white snow stuck to his goatee in multiple places.

"No one cares much about us, Miss…"

"Bridgestone. Call me Cassie."

Mrs. Hutchins nodded again. "No one bothers with us. Except our landlord, of course. I bet this is the answer to all his problems."

"What do you mean?"

"He wants us out." Judd lunged forward to grab a third doughnut.

"Why?" Cassie surveyed the unkempt state of the room and suspected she knew the answer but decided to go down the rabbit hole anyway.

"He wants to tear the house down. Our home—and he wants to destroy it."

"Really? Why would he do that?"

"Probably to grow some more of that weed he's harvesting." Mrs. Hutchins slammed her fist on the arm of the chair.

Judd briefly choked on his doughnut and coughed to clear his throat.

"Weed, like marijuana?" Cassie asked.

"Yup. The eviction process ain't working fast enough for him. We got no plans to budge, but now with Lloyd gone, I got no choice."

Mrs. Hutchins's eyes glistened with tears, and Cassie suddenly remembered that a hurting soul sat in front of her. What had happened affected more people than just Zach and Anna. She leaned forward and put her hand on Mrs. Hutchins's bony knee. "I'm so sorry. Do you have any idea where you'll go?"

Mrs. Hutchins shook her head and rocked her chair. A mangy cat walked in the room and brushed against Cassie's leg. She reached down to scratch its flea-bitten head.

"Don't worry, Ma." Judd wiped crumbs off his pants and let them land on the floor. "You know I got big business plans. I'll get us set up somewhere real nice."

"Oh?" Cassie turned her attention to Judd. "What kind of business plans?"

Behind the scraggly hair on his face, Judd's cheeks turned a different shade of pink. "I've been, uh, lookin' at an opportunity. Just need to secure me a chunk of cash to start it up."

"Stop talkin' 'bout that, Judd. The lady here ain't interested." She shot Judd a warning look. "Thanks for offerin' your condolences and bringing the doughnuts. That was awfully nice of you."

Cassie took her cue to leave and stood. "You're very welcome. Again, I'm sorry for your loss."

Mrs. Hutchins nodded, and Judd leaned forward to grab another doughnut. Cassie showed herself out.

Chickadees chirped, and Cassie found the birds flitting about in the trees at the edge of the yard. She smiled at their presence and wiped some cat hair off her pants before getting into the car. The chickadees weren't all she had to smile about. Her short conversation with the Hutchins's ended up being quite fruitful. She ran the conversation through her head as she drove back into the village.

A mean landlord wanted to speed up the eviction process in order to grow more marijuana on his land.

She now had a suspect and a motive.

She had to tell Lexy.

Chapter 9

"I can't believe you actually came away from the Hutchinses' with a suspect!" Lexy blurted through the phone.

"Not so loud! I don't want ol' flatfoot to hear you!" Cassie held her phone in one hand and drummed her fingers on the steering wheel of her parked car with the other.

"You could've texted, you know." Lexy sighed. "Unless... you want me to take a look at the records in the municipal office, don't you? To find out who the landlord is."

"What a great idea!" Cassie grinned at herself in the rearview mirror.

"Very funny. I'll do it when Welby leaves for lunch."

"Thanks, Lex!"

"What are you doing now?"

"I'm at the store."

"The store, huh?" Lexy's voice dripped with sarcasm.

"Yes, why?"

"Your store?"

"Of course, my store. What other store would I be in?" Cassie furrowed her brows.

"Oh, I don't know—a bookstore, perhaps?"

Cassie's cheeks warmed, and she was grateful Lexy couldn't see her through the phone. "Not funny."

"It wasn't supposed to be!" But Lexy laughed anyway. "Have fun! I'll let you know what I find."

"Thanks." Cassie hung up and stared at the back of her building. She wanted to check on Daniel, but now she felt guilty about it—like she'd be giving into Lexy's wily suggestion if she did.

She shook her head and grabbed her purse from the passenger seat. Daniel didn't need checking on again. There was absolutely no reason for her to go and see him right now. She opened the door and stepped out of the SUV onto the gravel lot. As she swung the door shut, her purse strap snagged and went with it.

Cassie tugged, but it was wedged tightly in the door. Sighing, she opened the door to pull the strap out and shut it again. Tossing the strap over her head to rest on her shoulder, she whirled around to see Daniel leaning against the corner of the building, his arms crossed and a big grin stretched across his face.

"Aren't you going to lock that?" He uncrossed his arms briefly to point at the SUV. Cassie's eyes were drawn to the flexed muscle in his forearm. She tried to will the heat in her cheeks to dissipate as she approached him.

"Lock what, the vehicle?" Cassie laughed. "You *are* a city slicker."

Daniel stopped holding up the wall with his shoulder and joined her steps in rhythm as she rounded the corner of the building.

"You're serious, aren't you?" One of his eyebrows lifted slightly higher than the other.

"You have a lot to learn about small towns." Cassie lightly punched his shoulder.

"I guess I do. Are you offering to teach me?"

"Maybe. How's the store coming along?" They stopped in front of the entrance. Above the door hung a newly-installed sign with painted wooden letters. "The Book Nook. I love it! Clever name."

"Thanks."

Beyond the Opening Soon sign in the window, a few rustic crates and well-placed books made up a display in the large windowsill. "That looks nice, too. I see you have a creative side."

Daniel snickered. "I guess you could say that!" He gently touched her arm and then shoved his hand into his jeans pocket. His nice-fitting jeans. "Seriously. Are you willing to teach me more about this small town of yours?"

"You mean, like a tour?"

"Exactly."

"Oh, um…" Cassie looked at her bare wrist. She never wore a watch. Why did she do that? She pulled out her phone from her back pocket to check the time.

"Unless you're too busy, of course." Daniel took a small step back.

"No, no—uh…" She returned the phone to her pocket.

"What about tonight? About seven?"

"Perfect. Where should we meet?"

Cassie's heart fluttered. Why was she so nervous? This was not acceptable. She took a deep breath to calm her nerves. She tried to make it look like she was thinking instead of trying to maintain her composure. Why shouldn't she show him around? He was new to the area and needed help. There was nothing wrong with that. "I'll come by your place to get you. Will that work?"

"Sure. I'll see you then." Daniel winked and flashed his charming smile.

Her legs were like rubber. She grinned like a lovesick fool as he turned and entered his store. After another deep breath, Cassie willed her legs to move forward and around the corner to the front of the building and her own store entrance.

"I'm back!" Cassie pulled her purse strap over her head and dumped the purse behind the counter. Pumpkin chirped and stood on her bed. She arched her back and stretched her front paws far out. "Hi, kitty bear!" Cassie scratched the cat's head, and she purred.

"Hi. Why'd you come in the front?" Maggie stopped stocking the candle display and looked over her shoulder at Cassie.

Why did she come in the front? Blast that Daniel Sawyer. He was confounding her brain. "I was, uh, checking the window displays."

Maggie continued stocking the shelf. Cassie was relieved she seemed satisfied with that answer. "Has it been busy this morning?"

"Steady. This is the first time there's been a lull." Maggie placed the last candle on the shelf and turned around. She wiped her hands on her pants as she approached Cassie at the counter.

Cassie pressed a couple of computer keys and watched the daily sales figure pop up on the screen. "Wow, that's more than steady!"

"Fishing tournament wives." Maggie smiled. "Big shoppers."

"I'm counting on it." Cassie cleared the number from the screen. "Hey, I have a few other errands to run. You okay if I duck out for a couple more hours after your lunch?" She hoped Lexy would have the landlord information back to her by then.

Maggie glanced at the antique clock on the wall. "No problem. Everything okay?"

Cassie loved how well her sister-in-law could read her. "Yes. I want to follow up on a couple leads."

A frown developed on Maggie's face. "I know you want to help Zach and Anna—"

"And Ida and Bubba."

"And Ida and Bubba." Maggie nodded. "But please be careful. I don't think this is something you should really get involved in. Let the cops do their job, Cassie."

"I would, *if* they were actually doing their job. That's the problem." She sighed and tidied the stack of gift bags behind the cash counter. "Besides. I'm not doing anything drastic. I wouldn't even know how."

Maggie grabbed her purse and walked around the counter. "If I know you, you'll find a way." She raised her eyebrows and gave Cassie a soft glare.

Cassie laughed. "Enjoy your lunch, Maggie. Bring me back a bagel."

"Always do!" Maggie pushed the door open and stepped out to the street, the bell clanging against the glass pane as the door shut behind her.

With only two customers in the rear of the store, Cassie took advantage of the moment, rested her elbows on the counter, and propped up her chin. What was she doing? Why was she the one who agreed to help Ida and the others? What did she know about solving a murder? Pumpkin jumped on the counter beside her. Cassie absentmindedly petted her as she thought through the problem.

On the other hand, she surmised, she probably knew a lot more about solving murders than the others. Cassie had years of experience reading mystery books and watching BBC cozy mystery shows. And even though they were all fiction, they made her think differently than most people.

She was just the person to help. And maybe the only one who could.

Her phone vibrated in her pocket. Cassie pulled it out and saw Lexy's number. She quickly glanced at the customers. One woman now stood at the candle display, opening and sniffing every single candle, and the other was taking her time selecting the right gingham- patterned tea towels.

Cassie swiped to answer her phone and placed it to her

ear. "Did you find anything?"

"Hello! How are you?" Lexy chided.

"Yeah, sorry. Hi. Did you find anything?" Pumpkin plopped her plump body on the counter so Cassie would scratch her belly. She obliged.

"Ross Sheffield owns the property where the Hutchinses live. He also owns three other rental homes."

"Ross Sheffield—the insurance guy?"

"Yes. There's nothing strange about his land ownership records, but he did have an application submitted to the office, dated a few months ago."

"Application for what?"

"A permit to demolish the home on the property where the Hutchinses live."

"Gladys mentioned that. At least we know it's true, now. Anything else on the application?" Cassie stopped petting Pumpkin and drummed her fingers on the counter. The cat nudged her, begging for more attention.

"In the reasons section, he listed he wants to convert it to agricultural use."

"I bet he does."

"It's still illegal to grow pot without a licence," Lexy added.

"Yes, but he can have more acreage to hide it on, get farming credits, and have less people around to find it."

"That's a motive to hurry up the eviction then, isn't it?"

"I'd say so. I'm going to pay him a visit. I think I have an insurance policy I'd like a second opinion on." Cassie pushed Pumpkin off the counter as the candle-sniffing woman approached with three candles. "I've gotta run. Thanks for this, Lex!"

"Glad to help. I wish I could go with you to see him. I don't like you going alone."

"I'll be fine. It's a public office."

"It was also a public river where Lloyd Hutchins was murdered."

"Point taken." Cassie gulped as she hung up.

Chapter 10

An electronic bell chimed as Cassie pushed open the front door of the red-brick N.D. Draycott Insurance building. She tucked her hair behind her ear as she approached the petite blonde behind the reception desk.

"Welcome! How can I help you today?" Her eyes sparkled, and her pixie haircut made Cassie wonder if she might be hiding wings under her dress blazer.

"Hi. I'm wondering if Ross Sheffield is available? I'd like to talk to him about changing my rental property policy."

"No problem," her voice sang. "Let me see." She clicked her mouse a number of times while staring at the large computer screen in front of her.

Cassie took the opportunity to look around the room. A few black chairs lined the wall between tall palm-leafed plants. Two hallways stretched out on each side behind the reception desk.

A whiteboard on the back wall showed whether the

agents were in or out of the office. Ross Sheffield's name was at the top. He was in. Two other brokers were in, and one was out.

"Hmm..." The receptionist propped her chin up with her hand and gave Cassie an apologetic smile. "It looks like he has an online meeting coming up soon. But Jack is available. Can I get your name?"

"Cassie Bridgestone." Cassie reached out her hand. "I own the Olde Crow Primitives store around the—"

"I thought I recognized you! I'm Alyssa." She eagerly grasped Cassie's hand and shook it. "I love your store!"

"Thanks! I think I remember seeing you in there," Cassie lied. "I didn't realize you worked so close by."

"Everyone's close by in Banford!" Alyssa laughed. "Hey, do you have any more of those small, metal stars? I'm making a keepsake box for my mother, and I need about six of them." She held her fingers about two inches apart to show Cassie the size.

"I should have enough. When I head back to the store, I'll put them aside for you."

Alyssa's eyes lit up again. "Thank you!" She looked over her shoulder and lowered her voice. "I've been instructed to throw some more clients Jack's way, but I'll get you in to see Ross. His conference doesn't start for another thirty minutes, so he should have time to squeeze you in."

"Thank you. I really appreciate it." Cassie smiled as Alyssa winked at her.

"Just have a seat, and I'll be right back." Alyssa turned down the hallway to the left.

Cassie chose one of the chairs but had barely sat down before Alyssa was back in the room with Ross Sheffield at her side. He had on an old, grey suit that needed to be pressed. His graying hair was slicked back, and Cassie noticed he could do with a shave.

An uneasy feeling in her gut warned her not to trust this guy.

"Miss Bridgestone, I'm Ross." He held his hand out to her.

She stood and reciprocated the handshake, his too-firm grip adding to her immediate dislike of the man. She tried not to wrinkle her nose as she caught the faint odor of cigarette smoke.

"Hi!" Cassie swallowed her pride and flipped her hair over her shoulder. "Nice to meet you." His grin turned her stomach.

"After you." He held his hand out toward the hallway. "I'm the second door on the right."

As Cassie stepped in front of him, she caught his eyes lowering to check out her backside. She pulled her shirt farther down over her khaki shorts.

She took a seat in the office as he returned to his desk.

"So, what can I do for you?"

"I'm looking to change up my rental property policy." Cassie leaned forward and examined his eyes. Her mother, Sandra, always told her you could tell a lot about a person by looking into their eyes. She often quoted the Bible verse about them being the window to a person's soul. Cassie saw darkness in Ross's eyes.

"We can certainly look into that. What are you wanting to change?"

Cassie swallowed. "I understand you own rental property, Mr. Sheffield?"

He leaned back into his chair. "Yes, I do. I own a few properties, why?"

"I'm looking for your expertise. I'm having trouble with a tenant who's not paying rent, and I want to evict them, but I think they're going to give me a hard time. Is there insurance that would help me cover the rental income in the meantime?"

He propped his foot across his opposite knee and twisted a pen in his hand. Cassie tried not to grimace at the dog hair on his sock.

"I understand your dilemma. I'm currently in the same situation myself."

"Really?" Cassie raised her eyebrows and twisted a lock of hair around her finger.

"Yes. Not the lack of payment but an eviction, nonetheless. It's actually quite hard to evict tenants in Ontario. The process can easily take six months, going through the proper channels." Ross's eyes twitched.

Cassie leaned forward more and lowered her voice. "Are there any... improper channels I could take? Possibly?"

Ross's closed-mouth smile stretched out to one side as he put his leg down and mimicked Cassie's movement of leaning forward. "I wouldn't know about that."

Cassie thought back to all the mystery novels she'd read.

The sleuth always had quick wit and knew what to say. Clearly that wasn't real life.

"Maybe you could tell me a bit more about your situation. That might help me."

Ross furrowed his brows and sat back again. "There's not much to tell. I have a property with acreage and an old house on it. The tenants have been there for years and pay diddly-squat in rent. Of course, I'm stuck with the provincial laws of only tiny rent increases each year, and it's not making me any money."

"I hear you on that one." Cassie nodded, even though she didn't really have an opinion about provincial rent increase restrictions.

"I'm trying to evict them, but they're paying rent, so I can only do it under the change-of-use clause. It takes forever. I plan to tear the house down and start growing soybeans on the property instead. Do you know how much you can make growing soybeans these days?"

Cassie fought the urge to roll her eyes. Soybeans. Yeah, right. But she saw an in, and she wasn't going to give up the chance. "Wait a sec, are you talking about the Hutchinses' property by the river?"

Ross's eyes narrowed slightly. She'd have to tread carefully. "You know the Hutchinses?"

"No, not at all." She waved her hand like it was no big deal. "But I heard about him drowning yesterday. Wasn't that awful?"

"Yes, I guess it was."

"But that will help you evict them now, right?"

"How do you figure, Miss Bridgestone?" He tossed his pen on the desk.

Cassie's efforts weren't working. How hard could she press before he closed up altogether? She decided to play dumb. "Oh, it doesn't? I don't know. I'm just asking."

Ross dropped his shoulders. "It might make a difference if they aren't able to pay their rent now. And without him there to help run the property, they might be more easily convinced to move elsewhere sooner."

Cassie leaned in again. "But in reality, it's already too late for this year, isn't it? So, what's the hurry?"

"What do you mean?"

"Soybean planting happens in May. It's already June. You can't plant until next year now, anyway. So why not let them stay the winter?"

Ross crossed his arms. "I thought you were coming to me for advice, Miss Bridgestone. Sounds like you're trying to give it instead."

"I'm trying to understand, is all." Cassie twirled her hair again. She was losing him. "Why the urgency?"

"The urgency is that they've been hemming and hawing and taking advantage of me for way too long!" Ross uncrossed his arms and slapped his hand on the desk. Cassie jumped. He grabbed the pen again and jabbed the desk with it as he spoke. "I started eviction proceedings in December. I should have a healthy crop of soybeans growing on that property right now! Instead, I have to waste this year and settle for growing fall rye."

"Are you sure this is really about soybeans?" Cassie

crossed her arms this time.

"What do you mean by that?"

"I've heard about the marijuana. Are you really upset about missing the soybean planting? Or are you worried about getting caught in your real enterprise?"

"Marijuana?" He pushed his chair back and jumped to his feet. "You have a lot of nerve!"

Cassie rose too. There was no way she was going to let him tower over her. "I might have nerve, but you have motive."

"Motive? Are you kidding me? Get out of my office!" He pointed at the door.

"Fine. I'll leave, but I'll be coming back with the cops."

"Is everything all right in here?" Alyssa poked her head in the door and glanced back and forth between Ross and Cassie.

"Get her out of here," Ross ordered. "And shut my door behind you."

"Yes, sir." Alyssa held the door for Cassie.

"And thanks, Miss Bridgestone." Ross sat again. "If there really is marijuana on that property, I can definitely speed up the eviction." He sneered.

Cassie glared back at him and imagined herself saying something clever. As usual, nothing came to mind, so she stayed silent.

"What was all that about?" Alyssa asked as she motioned for Cassie to lead the way up the hall.

"Ross owns the land the Hutchins family lives on."

"As in Lloyd Hutchins? The man who drowned

yesterday?" Alyssa slipped behind the counter and took a seat at her desk. Cassie stepped around to the front.

"The man who was murdered, yes."

"So awful." Alyssa shook her head. "But what does it matter if Ross owns the property?"

Cassie wasn't sure how much to say. On the other hand, maybe Alyssa would be a good source of information. "I thought maybe, you know, he might…"

"Might what?"

Clearly, she wasn't getting the hints. She'd have to spell it out for her. "Might be responsible for his death."

Alyssa laughed. Not the reaction Cassie expected. "Ross? No way. He can't even empty the mousetrap. I have to do it."

"But if he had motive?"

"It wouldn't matter anyway. He was here all morning yesterday." Alyssa lifted a small stack of printed statements out of a bin and tapped the edges lightly on the desk to straighten the pile.

"The murder happened between seven and eight o'clock. Surely he wasn't here yet."

"Actually, he was. We both were. We came in at six to reorganize the back room and get an office ready for a broker who's being transferred here."

"Oh." Cassie's shoulders slumped. She'd been certain Ross was guilty. There went her one and only good lead.

Alyssa leaned forward and whispered again, "But if you're looking for suspects, you might want to know that a certain Gladys Hutchins took out a rather hefty life insurance policy against her husband about a month ago."

"Really?" Cassie's eyes opened wide.

"But you didn't hear it from me."

Sometimes, Cassie mused, small town gossip was beneficial.

Chapter 11

"It makes sense." Lexy sat on the stool at Cassie's kitchen counter, holding a cup of hot tea between her hands. "They're being evicted and probably have no place to go. If the rent was low, as Ross claimed, they wouldn't be able to afford to move anywhere else. She needed the money."

"Clearly Gladys couldn't have done it herself." Cassie leaned back against the opposite counter, sipping tea from her mug. "So how would she convince Judd to kill his father?"

"Maybe he didn't need convincing. Maybe Lloyd found out about the pot and threatened to turn him in."

"Or maybe Gladys promised Judd a portion of the insurance money. He did mention something about a business venture he was interested in."

Pumpkin mewed and rubbed up against Cassie's ankles. Cassie set her mug on the counter and bent down to pick up the cat and cradle her in her arms. Rolls of furry fat hung over the side of Cassie's forearm.

Lexy giggled. "Too many cat treats lately?"

Cassie glared at her friend and kept scratching Pumpkin's belly. The cat's purr roared like a race engine. "Or maybe Gladys doesn't even know Judd did it. Perhaps he decided to take advantage of the life insurance policy all on his own."

"But the money goes to Gladys, not Judd." Lexy grabbed the carton of creamer from the counter and added a bit more to her tea.

"I don't think it would be too hard for him to get it from her."

"I suppose." Lexy sighed. "So, what's our next step?"

Cassie put Pumpkin on the floor and grabbed her phone from her back pocket. "We have time to go to the Hutchinses' for a quick visit, as long as I'm back here by seven."

Lexy downed her tea and placed her mug on the counter. "Sounds good, except what's your excuse for going there twice in one day?"

"I don't know. I'll think of something. Although, if I bring more food, I probably won't be questioned." She shoved her phone back into her pocket. "Judd may or may not have murdered Lloyd, but he certainly murdered the doughnuts I brought him this morning!"

Lexy laughed as she stood and grabbed her purse from the counter. "How about I bring them something, and you give me a ride there. That can be your excuse."

"Sounds good." Cassie grabbed her keys from a hook by the door and gave Pumpkin another scratch on the head.

"I'll be back soon, sweetie!"

Pumpkin chirped in response.

Lexy stepped out first. "Why do you have to be back at seven?"

"Uh, no reason." Cassie turned to fidget with the lock on the door.

"Okay, what's going on?" Lexy stood in the stairwell with her hand on her hip, waiting.

"Nothing. Why do you ask?"

"First, you're avoiding my question. Second, you just locked your apartment door, and we're only going away for an hour or so."

Cassie pulled the keys back and headed down the stairs.

"And third, your face is red."

"It is not." Cassie stepped ahead of Lexy in an effort to hide her face.

"Oh!" Lexy gasped as they reached the landing. "It's Daniel!"

"What? Where?" Cassie whirled around and dropped her keys, for the forty millionth time that week.

"Ha! I knew it! You have a date!"

"No. No, I do not have a date."

"Yes, you do! You're going to see Daniel tonight!" Lexy let loose a tiny squeal.

"It's not what you think." Cassie continued down the last flight of stairs. "He just needs someone to show him around."

"Nice try, Cassie." Lexy followed her out the door and by Daniel's storefront. "Anyone can walk up and down the block once and see everything there is to see in this town. You like him!"

"Shh!" Cassie hurried past the bookshop and into the parking lot. "I'm being a good landlord."

"Mm-hmm." Lexy smirked and opened the vehicle passenger door. "I'm sure all landlords give town tours to their tenants."

"Oh, shush." Cassie climbed into the SUV.

"I'll shush, as long as you promise to give me all the details later." Lexy winked as she buckled her seat belt. "Don't forget to stop at the bakery."

Minutes later, a box of doughnuts sat on Lexy's lap as Cassie turned the vehicle down the dusty driveway to the Hutchinses' house. As they rounded a curve, Judd's truck came into view. The hood was up, and he fiddled with the engine. He looked up as Cassie parked beside him.

"Hi, Judd." Cassie and Lexy climbed out of the vehicle. "How are you doing?"

"All right." He eyed the doughnuts in Lexy's hand.

"This is my friend, Lexy."

Lexy held out her free hand to Judd.

He pulled his arms out of the engine, wiped some grease on his pants, and reached for her hand but stopped. "I don't think you want to shake my hand right now, miss. But I'm pleased to meet you."

"I'm sorry for your loss, Judd." Lexy held out the box of doughnuts, and he took them without hesitation.

"Thank you." He opened the box and grabbed a jelly-filled pastry.

"They're, uh, for your mom too." Cassie pointed into the box. "How is she doing? Is she here?"

"Yup." He turned to the house. "Hey, Ma!" Powder flew out of his mouth as he yelled.

Lexy pursed her lips together and avoided eye contact with Cassie. They'd have to laugh about it later.

Gladys appeared at the wooden screen door. "Yeah?"

"The doughnut woman is back." Judd started working on pastry number two.

She stepped out of the house and wiped her hands on her apron. "Again?"

"My friend Lexy wanted to offer her condolences." Cassie shifted her weight from one foot to the other as the old lady approached them. She hadn't given the potential awkwardness of coming twice in one day enough thought.

"Well, thanks." Gladys furrowed her brows and glanced back and forth between the girls.

Cassie felt a nudge in her spirit. Yes, she suspected them of murder, but what if they were innocent? These two lost their loved one the day before. She needed to be respectful. What would God want her to do if they weren't guilty?

"I know you don't really know me, but I'm here if you need any help." Cassie reached out to clasp Gladys's arm. "Please let me know if you need anything."

Judd set the doughnut box on the engine, tucked his head back under the hood, and twisted a wrench.

Gladys blinked a few times, and her twitching lips eventually stretched into a small smile. "Thank you kindly. But we're all right."

"I don't mean to pry." Lexy threw a quick glance at Cassie. "Will you have enough money to live without Lloyd?"

"We gotta move. But only because our darned landlord is making us." Gladys looked out over the yard. "I don't think I wanna be here without Lloyd, anyhow."

"Do you know where you'll go?" Cassie touched Gladys's arm again.

"Nah. But Lloyd and me, we got these life insurance policies on each other a few weeks ago. When the money comes through, I'll be able to find someplace."

"Life insurance?" Cassie wasn't going to let this opportunity slide by. "I'm so glad you have that. But why did you get it only a few weeks ago?"

Gladys crossed her arms. "My daughter made us. Glad she did, now."

"Daughter?" Cassie glanced at Lexy. It never occurred to her there might be another family member. A family member who'd just jumped onto her suspect list. "I didn't know you had a daughter."

"She lives out in BC with her little ones. I never see her. Though I expect she'll come home for Pa's funeral." Gladys looked into the sky. "Poor girl. That's two funerals in two months."

"Two? Who else?" Lexy jumped in.

"Her father-in-law. Up and had a heart attack, left his wife with nuthin'. That's why she insisted we get life insurance."

So not a new suspect after all. Cassie glanced over at

Judd, who continued to fidget under the hood of his truck. "What about Judd?" She lowered her voice and directed the question to Gladys. "Is he going to be all right?"

Gladys didn't catch the implied discreetness and blurted out her answer in a normal voice. "Judd's fine. He's been doing real good at work, and he's got all kinds of money he's been saving."

Judd's wrench slipped and banged the side of the engine with a loud clunk. He emerged from his hiding spot under the hood and turned to Gladys. "Easy there, Ma. That's private information."

"You were the one tryin' to tell her about your enterprise this mornin'!"

Judd set the wrench on the edge of the truck. "Yeah, but that don't involve talking about the money."

"What enterprise, Judd?" Lexy asked.

"Yes." Cassie turned to face him. "I'd love to hear about it. What are your plans?"

He stood a bit taller and stepped toward the girls. "I'm going to buy myself a garage. I've almost got my mechanic's hours in at Brown's to complete my apprenticeship, and I been getting all kinds of experience. As soon as I get my licence, I wanna open my own place."

"That's great!" Cassie smiled at him. He beamed back in return.

"Quite the business venture." Lexy tilted her head. "You'd need a lot of capital to get started, though. You must have been saving for quite a while."

"He's got loads of cash." Gladys uncrossed her arms

and turned to give her son a proud smile.

"Ma!" Judd glared at her.

"What? I'm proud of ya!" She turned back to the girls. "He does a great job and customers give him big tips all the time. Plus, he does a few side jobs Mr. Brown don't know about." She winked.

"Stop tellin', Ma." Judd's face grew red. "You gonna get me in trouble."

"Don't worry, Judd." Cassie waved her hand. "No big deal. And we won't tell. Right, Lex?"

"Right. Secret's safe with us," Lexy added.

"I thank you ladies for coming and for bringing me more of them doughnuts." Judd pointed to the box under the hood. Clearly, they had now outstayed their welcome.

"Yes, thank you." Gladys's eyes teared up as she clasped Cassie's hand in both of her own and gave Lexy a big grin.

Cassie's own eyes watered a little. "You're welcome, Gladys. And please, give me a call if you need anything. I have connections at the church if you need help with funeral planning or catering—anything at all."

Gladys squeezed her lips together and nodded. She let go of Cassie's hands, turned, and rushed back into the house.

Cassie turned to Judd, who had once again disappeared under the truck hood. "Don't worry, Judd. We won't tell anyone about the side work you're doing at Brown's."

"But that's not where you're getting all the money, is it?" Lexy chimed in.

Cassie whipped her head around and glared at Lexy.

What was she doing? "Time to go, Lexy."

"What do ya mean by that?" Judd emerged from the engine, the wrench gripped firmly in his hand.

"No one makes loads of cash from tips and mechanic side jobs." Lexy, clearly a foot shorter than Judd, had no qualms about taking a step forward and challenging him.

"It's none of your business how I get my money." He pointed the wrench down the driveway. "Time for you to go."

"Sorry, Judd." Cassie tugged on Lexy's shirt sleeve. "Enjoy the rest of the doughnuts."

"What are you doing?" Lexy whispered as she and Cassie climbed into the SUV.

"Leaving."

Cassie turned the vehicle around and waved at Judd as they drove by. He continued to stare at them, the tool clenched in his hand.

"I was getting close!" Lexy lightly slapped her legs in frustration.

"Close to setting him off. What if he's innocent, Lexy? He lost his father yesterday." Cassie turned onto the main road.

"And what if he's guilty?"

"Then you would have been challenging a murderer." Cassie glanced in her rearview mirror. Judd's truck pulled out of the driveway behind them. "A murderer who's now following us."

Chapter 12

"Still think he might be innocent?" Lexy looked over her shoulder at Judd's truck, following at a safe distance behind Cassie's SUV.

Cassie studied her rearview mirror but couldn't make out Judd's facial expressions. She turned onto the street leading into town. "I don't know. What would be the point of following us if he was guilty? He knows where my shop is."

"Intimidation." Lexy leaned forward and watched the sideview mirror. "He turned. He's still following."

Cassie quickly braked and pulled into the next side street on her right. "How about now?"

Lexy turned around. "Nope. He drove by. Do you think he missed seeing us turn?"

"No. I think he wasn't actually following us." Cassie drove around the block and back onto the main road. "Our imaginations are getting the better of us."

"Yeah, it's not like there was a murder or anything."

Lexy playfully punched Cassie's arm. "Hey. There's his truck." She pointed to the parking lot of Brown's Garage as they drove past.

"He may not have been following us, but he's definitely my lead suspect." Cassie drove across the swing bridge, turned right, and pulled into the lot behind her building. "Coming up for another tea?"

The girls climbed out of the vehicle, but Lexy grabbed her keys and headed to her own car. "Nope. You have a date to get ready for." She winked. "But I'll definitely be talking to you soon."

"It's not a date!" Cassie spoke in a hushed tone but raised her head high. "But I do have to get ready."

Lexy laughed and climbed into her car. "Have fun!"

Cassie waved and ran into the building and up to her apartment.

"Rowr!" Pumpkin greeted her.

"Hi, sweetie!" Cassie offered the cat her usual head scratch and glanced at her phone. She had forty minutes before she had to meet Daniel. She scooped Pumpkin into her arms and rushed off to the bedroom. She gently set the cat onto her bed and took a look at herself in her full-length mirror.

She bit her bottom lip and ran her fingers through her hair. Should she shower again? Or just get changed? And what should she wear? Cassie opened her closet door and rummaged through a few outfits, pushing them aside one by one because they were too dressy, too frumpy, too old, or too unflattering.

Cassie sighed and plopped herself down on the edge of the bed. Pumpkin trilled at her and rubbed her head against Cassie's arm.

"What's the big deal, Pumpkin?" She scratched her soft head again, and the cat flopped on her side. "I never care what I wear. What is happening to me?"

The cat merely responded with a loud purr. Cassie shook her head, hoping to regain her senses, and decided to get ready for her non-date without a fuss.

A half hour later, Cassie stood outside Daniel's apartment in cute jean shorts and a white lacy tank top with blue flowers. She'd pulled her hair into a ponytail and let a few wisps hang down the sides of her face. Nothing too special, but she felt good.

She knocked on the door and waited until Daniel opened it. He took her breath away. He had on plaid shorts with different tones of grey, and a tight grey T-shirt. The short sleeves hugged his biceps.

"Hi!" His eyes sparkled as he smiled at her.

"Hi," Cassie replied softly. She swallowed to find her voice. "Ready for the tour?"

"Absolutely." He pulled the door shut and started to lock it, but before he turned the key, he looked at Cassie.

She laughed. "It's okay. I won't make fun of you if you lock your door."

He turned the key, and the lock clicked. "As long as you're sure." He stood tall and grinned at her again.

"I understand you're a city boy. Old habits die hard."

"I'm willing to learn country-hick ways, if you'll teach

me." He put his hand on the small of her back as they walked toward the stairs.

Cassie swore she felt a jolt of electricity from his touch. "Hick? Who are you calling a hick?" She laughed and tried to ignore the flip-flopping of her stomach as they descended the stairs and stepped out onto the street.

"It's a beautiful evening." Daniel took a deep breath. "I can't get over how fresh the air is here."

"I don't know how people breathe in the city." Cassie led the way to the front corner of her building.

"It's a talent."

Cassie laughed. "This is the main intersection. Most everything you'll need is either along First Avenue"—Cassie pointed down the street that followed the river and then turned and pointed at the street heading through town—"or here on Main Street."

"It must be a busy intersection. It has the only traffic light in town."

"Very funny. Except the light is only here because of the swing bridge. And it's not actually in this intersection." Cassie pointed at the light, hanging north of the corner. "It's only ever red if there are boats going through."

"And here I thought I'd just been lucky to always get green lights."

Cassie smirked. "Why don't we go up and down Main here, and then we can walk by the water?"

"You're the boss." Daniel lightly brushed the small of her back again.

Cassie inhaled quickly at his touch and held her breath

until he let go a few seconds later. He followed her down the sidewalk.

"Drummond's Bakery and Deli makes the best pastries and sandwiches." She pointed across the street at the restored, old building with the decorative storefront. Next to that stood a slew of stores, all with painted wooden storefronts and big display windows. "And then you have Snow Dragon Ice Cream Shop, Java Junction, Candle Barn, and Charming Treasures."

"I see." He nodded.

Cassie looked at the ground. "I guess you can read signs. You probably don't need me to tell you that."

"No, no." He continued studying the stores. "This is good. There are a lot of cute shops in this town."

Cassie giggled.

"What?" Daniel tilted his head.

"Cute? We can go shopping later if you like."

Daniel playfully swatted her arm. "Very funny."

She loved the banter between them. He made her laugh, and she felt her heart opening up more toward him. But she needed to strengthen her resolve. This wasn't a date, and he wasn't a potential mate. This was a simple town tour for one of her tenants. She willed her heart to stop behaving so erratically.

A red-haired woman walked out of a store ahead of them. "Hi, Cassie!"

"Hey, Dierdre. How are you?"

"Good, thanks!" She hopped in a car parked along the side of the street.

Daniel grinned at Cassie.

"What?"

"Nothing. Small towns." He continued grinning. She chose to ignore it.

They walked silently for a few moments, taking in the sights. She pointed out the Kettle Kitchen and made sure to let him know about their famous mustards and jellies. She showed him The Tea Garden, where she often met Maggie and Lexy for morning tea. They passed the Wood Oven Pizza parlour, Daffodilly Flower Shop, and Alley Cat Yarn Shop.

"And Hardcastle's is my favourite restaurant." Cassie pointed out the old, three-storey stone building across the street. Red geraniums bloomed in the window boxes below the tall, paned windows, and an old red phone booth stood at the corner. The far wall was covered in vines. It looked like a scene transplanted straight from the Cotswolds in England. "My Gramma Merrick and I have breakfast there every Sunday before church."

Daniel looked at her, not at the building. "You know, your eyes light up when you talk about her. She must be quite special to you."

"She is." Cassie stared at the sidewalk and continued walking. She lightly kicked a pebble with the front of her flip-flop. "We're very close. My mom, Sandra, passed away when I was eighteen. She was Grams's daughter." Why was she telling him this? This was information reserved for her closest friends and family—she didn't discuss it with just anybody. She resisted the urge to explore the possibility that

Daniel might not be "just anybody." He was slowly tapping through the walls around her heart.

"I'm sorry." Daniel touched her back again. "That must have been hard."

"It was. It still is. I miss my mom like crazy. Everything I am today is because of her. She was wise, kind, and loved God with a fierceness I could only hope to have, one day."

Daniel dropped his hand. "I'm glad you're close with your grandmother. What about your dad?"

"He remarried and lives in the next town. I see him regularly, along with my brother, Rick. His wife, Maggie, works in my store. She's one of my best friends."

"Ah, yes. I've seen her."

"Let's cross." Cassie waited for a boat and trailer to pass before stepping out into the street and crossing to the other side. Daniel followed.

"Wait until you see this street at Christmas time." Cassie pointed toward the cute shops. "The town and the shops go all out with their decorations and cute Christmas things. People come from all over for the Christmas Festival and the Holiday Train."

"The Holiday Train comes through Banford?" Daniel asked, referring to the train decked out in Christmas lights that travelled across Canada at Christmas time. It stopped in towns to give concerts from one of the train cars.

"We're a special town." Cassie beamed.

"I'm learning that, very quickly." They passed by the Snow Dragon Ice Cream Shop again. "Do you want a cone? My treat."

"Sure! I never say no to ice cream!" Cassie followed him into the cute, fifties-style ice cream shop. Two adults, two teenagers, and a child stood ahead of them in line. One of the teens turned and waved at Cassie. It was one of the youths from her church. She returned the wave.

The music was a bit loud to enjoy conversation, so Cassie and Daniel waited in silence, looking around at the fun décor. When it was finally their turn, Cassie shouted out her order of one scoop of strawberry on a waffle cone to the teenager behind the counter.

"Really?" Daniel spoke above the music. "All these flavours and you pick plain strawberry?"

"I know what I like. What are you getting?"

The teen handed Cassie her cone and looked to Daniel for his order.

"I'll have two scoops please. One of maple walnut, and the other Moose Tracks."

"Blech." Cassie laughed. "Is that the Canadian special?"

"I know what I like." Daniel grinned.

Moments later, they licked their cones and continued down the sidewalk. As they passed The Blackhorse Inn and Restaurant, Jake and Mitch, the two fishermen renting her apartment, came out the door.

"Hey, guys!" Cassie waved.

"Oh, hey there, Cassie." Mitch said.

"How's the fishing going?"

"Good." Jake adjusted the cap on his head. "Looking to be a nice day tomorrow too."

"I'm glad." Cassie took a quick lick of her cone. "Is the

apartment good? Do you have everything you need? Sorry I didn't check on you sooner."

"It's perfect." Mitch smiled. "We're enjoying our stay."

"I'm glad. Good luck tomorrow!" She waved as they continued across the street and chided herself for not checking in with them sooner. She was usually on top of her vacation apartment rentals, but with everything going on, she'd forgotten all about it. It was a good thing she'd run into them. She'd have to call the other tenant later.

"Huh. Busy town for fishing, busy town for Christmas, and busy town in the summer." Daniel watched the two men walk down the sidewalk and enter the door at the side of Cassie's building. "Are you sure you don't regret renting to me on a monthly basis, instead of keeping up the additional vacation apartment?"

"The jury hasn't come back on that one yet." Cassie giggled. "C'mon. Let me show you the river. Maybe we'll see a boat go through the locks."

"Locks? How many are there?" Daniel raised an eyebrow.

"Banford lock station has three sets." Cassie pointed at the locks beside the swing bridge and the two others a bit more downriver. "Have you ever seen locks at work?"

"No. But I'd love to." Daniel picked up his pace. "Let's check it out."

As luck would have it, a small yacht was being raised in one of the locks.

Daniel was fascinated at the old system of wooden locks and large iron wheels and chains that still functioned as efficiently as it had a hundred years ago. Bit by bit, the water poured through one side, until the level was the same as on the other side of the lock gate. Then the lockmaster turned the big wheel until the gate swung open and the boat could be on its way. The boat owner waved at the lockmaster as he passed him.

"Fascinating!" Daniel approached the nearest closed lock.

"Go across." Cassie prompted him, pointing at the three stairs leading to the top of the lock gate.

"What? Are you serious?" Daniel's mouth hung open.

Cassie laughed, rushed by him, and hopped up the stairs. "C'mon! It's not illegal."

Daniel tentatively followed her up the stairs. The top of the lock was only about two feet wide, with nothing but a single cross bar as a railing. "If you're sure." His eyes darted back and forth as he gripped the railing with one hand and his ice cream with the other.

The two lock gates met in the middle on an angle, leaving a slight opening in the walkway and an even larger gap between the railings on each gate. Cassie hopped across.

Daniel stared at her, still gripping the railing. "You want me to follow you there?"

Cassie laughed. "Is the city boy afraid of heights? It's not even high up here. The water is at the high level."

"I'm not afraid of heights." Daniel continued to grip the railing of the first lock gate. "I'm just not sure we're meant to do this."

"If you need help, I could ask her." Cassie pointed to

the next lock, upriver, as an elderly woman shuffled across it with her little poodle at the end of a lead.

Daniel rolled his eyes at Cassie. "Fine. I get your point." He jumped across and followed Cassie along the rest of the gate and down to the lawn on the other side.

"Good job!" Cassie patted him on the back. "Maybe tomorrow we'll try scaling Kilimanjaro."

"Funny one, aren't you?" Daniel wrinkled his nose at her.

"I've just never seen a—"

"Watch it!" Daniel grabbed Cassie as she tripped over a large mooring post. He pulled her away from the edge of the canal wall and managed to cushion her fall as she landed on him, instead of the hard ground.

Cassie stayed where she was for a moment, stunned by the fall, but more dazed by the fact she was so close to Daniel. He smelled like coffee and old books. Her stomach fluttered as she became aware of his strong arms, holding her tight. Her hand rested on his chest, and she gulped as the strong muscles tensed beneath her fingers. She stared into his eyes, and he returned her gaze.

"Are you all right?" He reached up with one of his hands and tucked her hair behind her ear.

"Yes." She breathed softly but still found herself unable to move.

"Still want to hike Kilimanjaro tomorrow?"

She dropped her forehead to his chest and laughed. "I think I'm good!" She pulled herself up and sat on the grass beside him. "Oh no!"

"What? What is it?" Daniel quickly sat up and studied her face.

"Our ice cream." Cassie pouted and pointed to the two cones, smooshed into the grass beside them.

Daniel fell back to the ground in a fit of laughter.

"C'mon. Let's go get some more!" Cassie stood and pulled on Daniel's arm to urge him to his feet. "This time it's my treat."

"Maybe I'll get tiger tail." Daniel licked his lips.

"Ew." Cassie shook her head.

This time they went to the swing bridge and walked across it on the sidewalk. Daniel looked down the river as they did so. "It must be beautiful out there."

"It is." Cassie nodded. "Have you never been out on the water?"

"Only Lake Ontario. In large boats, with lots of people. No place peaceful, like this. Do you have a boat?"

Cassie shook her head. "No, but I borrow a small one from Bubba's Bait Shop to check on a group of endangered sparrows nesting downriver."

Daniel stopped in the middle of the sidewalk and looked at her. "You check on endangered sparrows?"

"Uh, yeah." Cassie tucked her hair behind her ear and kept walking. "I'm a birder."

"A birder? What's that?" Daniel fell in step beside her again.

"A bird-watcher? A twitcher?"

Daniel snickered. "Okay, now that's something I didn't expect."

Cassie raised her chin. "It's quite fascinating and relaxing, actually."

"Don't get me wrong." Daniel placed his hand on her forearm. "I'm not making fun. It's interesting. Really interesting."

"Oh." Cassie slowed her pace as she relaxed. "I'm going early in the morning, if you'd like to join me."

"Really? I'd love that."

They crossed the intersection and headed to the Snow Dragon again. What was she doing? She shouldn't be spending so much time with Daniel. He wasn't a believer. He didn't love God the way he should. There was no future for them. Their lives could never be aligned. And even if they could be aligned, she wasn't ready, anyway.

But Cassie couldn't deny the longing in her heart.

She'd have to wrestle with God about it later.

Chapter 13

Cassie quickly downed her second cup of tea and left the mug on her counter. She shouldn't have had two teas already, but the alarm clock had blared a little too early for her liking, and she needed the extra boost.

Between thoughts of Daniel and thoughts about the murder, her sleep had been restless. On top of that, she wasn't a morning person. But the inconvenience was a sacrifice she'd always been willing to make to see as many of her feathered friends as possible.

She gave Pumpkin a quick cuddle, brushed the fur off her shirt, grabbed her backpack, and raced out the door. As she ran up the stairs to Daniel's apartment, she attempted to take them two by two, but her body wasn't quite awake enough, so she gave up after the first try.

Cassie took a moment outside Daniel's door to catch her breath and smooth her hair since the humidity was already attacking her curls. Today would not be a good hair day.

She tapped lightly on the door, and Daniel answered within seconds.

"You're here! Great! Let's go."

Cassie laughed at the sight before her. Daniel wore khaki shorts, a plain white T-shirt, a floppy camouflage-patterned hat, and rubber boots caked in dried mud.

"What's so funny?" Daniel looked down at his attire.

"Nothing. Nothing at all." Cassie smirked, looking at her own light-pink shirt and jean shorts. "You don't need rubber boots."

"But what if it's muddy?"

"We won't be getting out of the boat."

"Oh. Okay." As he kicked them off, clumps of dried mud landed on his floor.

"What on earth?" Cassie stared at the mess.

Daniel laughed. "On earth? I get it. Earth... as in dirt. Nice one!" He shoved his feet into a pair of nearby thonged sandals and jumped to her side.

"What?" Cassie shook her head. "Oh no. You're a morning person, aren't you?"

"You're not? Uh-oh. Do you need a coffee before we go?"

"No thanks. I only drink Earl Grey tea. And I've already had two cups. There's no bathroom on a fishing boat."

Daniel snickered. "Gotcha."

They made their way downstairs and out into the humid morning air. As they walked toward Bubba's, birds sang from the bushes along the riverside. The sun hung low in the sky, barely above the trees. It cast a warm glow on the water. A number of fishing boats dotted the river, full of eager fishermen trying for the big catch.

"Let me carry that for you." Daniel grabbed Cassie's backpack from her shoulder and threw it over his own. "Oof! What do you have in here?"

"It's my birding bag. I've got all my equipment in there."

"You need equipment to watch birds?"

"Of course." Cassie tucked her hair behind her ears as she continued down the sidewalk. "I've got my Sibley's bird book, my scope and a mini-tripod, two sets of binoculars—"

"Two sets?"

"I brought one for you."

"You own more than one set of binoculars?" Daniel raised his eyebrow at her.

"Well, yeah. I have four sets, actually. My good pair..." She counted off on her fingers. "My car pair, my mini pair, and my backup pair." She held four fingers in the air.

Daniel stared at her. "That's... fascinating."

Cassie narrowed her eyes and glared at him. "You better not be making fun of me."

"No, no." Daniel shook his head and waved his hands. "It's nice to know you're, uh, prepared."

She playfully swatted his arm. They arrived at Bubba's and turned on the sidewalk to his shop.

"Good morning, Cassie!" Bubba stopped hanging a bunch of trout lures on a rack and smiled. "And who do we have here?"

"This is Daniel Sawyer. He's opening the bookstore behind my shop."

"Nice to meet you. I'm Bubba Brooks." They shook hands. "Off to check on the sparrows, then?" Bubba grabbed another handful of lures to hang.

"Yes. I'm a bit worried about them with all the extra boat traffic from the tournament," Cassie said.

"Anna's coming in to give me a hand this morning, to help cover for Zach's... absence." He looked at the floor for a moment. "She should be here when you get back. I'm sure she'd love an update on the birds."

"Oh good." Cassie touched Bubba's arm until he made eye contact with her again. "How are you doing?"

Bubba's lips twitched behind his beard. "You know. Trying to keep busy with the tournament so I don't think too much about everything."

Cassie nodded and let go of Bubba's arm. "We're all praying, Bubba."

"Thanks." He stared at the floor again. "The keys are in the boat already."

"Thank you. We won't be long."

Daniel followed Cassie through the shop and out the back door marked for employees. "What is he so upset about?"

Cassie climbed into the aluminum fishing boat and untied the mooring knot. "His son Zach is the one accused of drowning Mr. Hutchins."

"Oh." Daniel removed his hat and scratched the back of his head. "I didn't realize. And he didn't do it?"

"No. He didn't. And his life is about to be ruined for nothing."

"That's awful." Daniel put his hat back on and stared into the boat. "How do I get into this thing?"

"Step down onto the bench. Use it like a stair."

Daniel did as instructed. The boat wobbled, so he quickly sat. "Now what?"

"Hang on." Cassie started the engine and pulled away from the dock. Once she passed the no wake zone, she released the throttle and took off down the river.

Daniel clapped one hand on his head to hold his hat on and held onto the bench with the other. Cassie smirked.

As they neared the nesting area, Cassie eased up on the throttle. She was disappointed to see a fishing boat nearby. She wasn't a competing fisherman, so the distance rules of how close she could go to the other boat didn't apply. However, she still wanted to respect the fishermen and gave them a wide berth, unlike Eric and Marjorie had for her and Anna the other day. Her jaw tightened as she recalled almost being capsized.

The boat bobbed in the water as she pulled a pair of binoculars out of the bag and handed them to Daniel. An osprey, holding a big fish in its talons, screeched overhead. Daniel quickly grabbed the binoculars and frantically searched the sky for the bird.

"Keep your eyes on the osprey, and then bring the binoculars in front of your face." Cassie grabbed her own pair and showed him. "It takes a bit to get the hang of it."

After a couple of tries, Daniel managed to focus on a

boat across the bay. "Wow. These work better than I thought they would!"

"And that's not even my good pair." Cassie smiled as she turned her binoculars onto the Henslow's sparrows' nesting site.

"Oh no!" Cassie turned the focus knob to get a clearer image.

"What's wrong?"

"The grass has been trampled along the shore. Someone has been on the nesting ground." She dropped her binoculars to her lap.

"Are the birds okay?" Daniel moved his binoculars around, trying to find the right spot.

"I don't see them. Let's move closer."

Cassie started the boat again and eased toward the shore. She waved at the nearby fishermen and moved slowly, trying not to disturb the fish. They waved back.

She waited until the boat was about a hundred feet from the shore and cut the engine. Then she picked up the oars and quietly rowed another few feet. Any closer and the birds wouldn't come out. Daniel found his focus and helped Cassie search the grassy field.

"Someone definitely walked there." Cassie sighed. "And I'm not seeing any movement around where the nests are."

"Be patient." Daniel put his hand on her knee. "I'm sure they're fine."

Cassie bit her lip as she continued to search the shore. Who would go there? Did a fisherman get his line caught and have to unsnag it? Were the birds scared away?

She fixated her binoculars on the nest site, waiting. Searching.

Everything stayed still. Her heart sank. What if the grass was trampled by a wild animal, like a fox or a coyote? The eggs could have been eaten.

Scenario after scenario raced through her mind as she scanned the area for any sign of the sparrows. She was worried about the birds, but it was nice to think of something else other than the murder. And Daniel.

She lowered her binoculars. Daniel sat on the boat floor, leaning back on the bench with his elbows propped behind him. He was watching her.

"What?" Cassie felt a bit of heat rise to her cheeks.

"Nothing. I'm admiring the scenery. It's really beautiful out here." He didn't remove his eyes from her.

Now her cheeks were really warm.

"Did you find the birds?" he asked.

"It's only been a few minutes. They might show yet." Cassie was hopeful.

"A few minutes?" Daniel looked at the big, shiny watch on his wrist. "You know you've been staring at that field for about a half hour, right?"

"Really?" Cassie shrugged. "You did tell me to be patient." Then her shoulders slumped. "I hope the birds are okay."

"Maybe they're out getting breakfast." Daniel pulled himself onto the bench again. "Whoa! Look at that!"

One of the fishermen in the next boat reeled in his line and drew a fish out of the water. After a few seconds, he unhooked it and threw it overboard.

"What? Why'd he do that? Aren't they in a contest?"

Cassie laughed. "They'll need a fish five times that size to win."

Daniel's eyes widened. "Really?"

"Really." Her smile quickly faded. "It's time to head back. I've got to tell Anna about the birds."

A short time later, Cassie steered the boat into the dock behind Bubba's. She rushed into the shop with Daniel at her heels. Anna was serving a customer at the cash register, so Cassie waved and waited for her to finish. When the customer left, Cassie dodged right to the counter.

"Anna. The birds aren't there! Someone's disturbed them!"

"What? How?" Anna came out from behind the counter.

"I don't know. The grass is all trampled. Daniel and I waited for a long time, but none of the birds showed up. There was no movement at all."

Anna swallowed. "I'm sure they're fine, Cassie."

"No. Something is wrong. I know it." Cassie rubbed her forehead. "I don't know if it was a fisherman, or a coyote, or what—but something disturbed them. I think we should call people from the bird club and alternate shifts guarding the shore. If they're still there, we want to give them the best chance for survival."

Anna looked around the store and back at Cassie. "Can I talk to you?" She grabbed Cassie's arm and glanced over at Daniel. "In private. Sorry."

Daniel shrugged and walked to a display of fishing rods. Anna dragged Cassie through the employee door and onto the back dock.

"What is it, Anna?" Cassie studied her friend's face, looking for any sign of what could be wrong.

"It was me, Cassie. I went on the shore."

"Why? When?"

Anna rubbed her face with her hand and continued. "On Thursday when I was out with Zach. I wanted to check on the birds, but Zach had no interest. We argued a bit about it, and I finally had him drop me off on the shore. I didn't go far, I promise. I stood near the edge and watched the birds from there."

"Were the birds there?"

"Yes. And they were fine when I left too."

"Why didn't you tell me before? Did you think I'd be mad?" Cassie spoke softly.

Anna took a deep breath and closed her eyes. "You know when Zach and I found Lloyd Hutchins's body?"

Cassie nodded. "Yes."

"Well, it wasn't me and Zach. It was just Zach."

"What?" Cassie took a few steps back and leaned against a railing. "I don't understand."

"It happened while I was on shore. I lied about being with him."

"Oh, Anna!"

"I didn't mean to. The cops assumed I was there. At first, I didn't think it mattered. I wanted to hide it, so Zach's fish wouldn't be disqualified because he was alone. And then they said it was murder. Suddenly, I became Zach's alibi. I thought it would help him, especially since he has a record."

"I can understand your reasons." Cassie sighed. "But you're going to have to tell the truth, Anna. You may be called upon to testify. You can't lie in court."

"I know." Anna chewed her bottom lip. "Oh, Cassie." A tear rolled down her cheek. "Zach can't be convicted of murder. He can't! You have to find the killer!"

"I'm working on it. I am." Cassie placed her hands on Anna's shoulders and looked her square in the eye.

"It's more important than you know." Anna's eyes filled with more tears.

"Why? What's aren't you telling me?"

"I'm pregnant, Cassie. My baby needs to know his father."

"Oh, Anna!" Cassie's heart melted as she pulled her friend into a hug. "How long have you known?"

"We just found out last week."

"I'll figure out who did this. You won't be alone."

Cassie stood there a few moments, letting Anna cry onto her shoulder. She thought about the weight of the promise she was making.

A promise she really hoped she could keep.

Anna pulled back and wiped the tears from her eyes.

Cassie checked her phone. "Can you get some time off in a couple of hours?"

"I think so. The biggest rush should be over by then. Why?"

"Would you like me to take you to see Zach?"

Anna let out a breath. "That would be great."

"Let me go open the store, and when Maggie comes in at eleven, I'll pick you up."

"Thank you. I'd really appreciate it."

Cassie pulled a teary Anna into a hug. "Okay then. I'll see you soon."

It would be good for Anna to visit Zach, and maybe, Cassie could get some more answers about what really happened to Lloyd.

Chapter 14

A few minutes after eleven o'clock, Cassie pulled her SUV into a parking spot along the street near Bubba's Bait Shop. A few boats bobbed along the public dock, no doubt belonging to tournament fishermen topping up their lure supplies before heading out for another round of fishing.

She grabbed her sunglasses from the dashboard and put them on, reducing the glare of the sun on the sparkling water. Tourists, and likely a lot of fishermen's wives, walked along the waterfront, enjoying the beautiful weather. Many of them had already wandered through Olde Crow Primitives that morning, but the store would remain busy all day. Cassie felt bad for stepping out again. Thankfully, Grams had offered to help Maggie for a few hours, but it wasn't the same as being there herself. She enjoyed serving the tourists who came through.

But right now, Anna needed her more. A visit with Zach would do the girl some good. Since Banford didn't have its own jail, Zach had been placed in a cell at the county provincial police station, twenty minutes up the highway. Anna didn't have her licence, and Cassie didn't think she should visit by herself, anyway.

As Cassie turned on the sidewalk to Bubba's, Anna walked out the front door. A backpack purse hung from her shoulder. She waved when she saw Cassie.

"I was watching for you." Anna caught up to Cassie.

"It's okay for you to leave? Bubba's not too busy in there?"

"He'll be fine for a bit. He wants me to see Zach." Anna forced a smile.

They climbed in the vehicle, and Cassie pulled out onto the street, around a big truck and boat trailer. "Have you been able to talk to him at all?"

Anna shook her head. "Not really. Just one quick phone call last night."

"How is he doing?" Cassie pushed her sunglasses into her hair and put the car visor down instead.

"He's scared. He keeps trying to explain what happened, but no one will listen to him." Anna sniffed. "And now I've made it worse by lying! When they find out, it'll make him look even more guilty." She turned to look out the window as they drove out of town and onto the quiet, two-lane highway.

Cassie patted Anna's leg a couple of times but struggled for something to say. Anna wasn't a believer in God, so a Bible verse or a quote about faith probably wouldn't do anything for her. She said a silent prayer for her friend instead, asking God to comfort Anna and to make His presence known in this situation. She also prayed for the real murderer to be brought to justice so the whole mess would go away.

"Are you really trying to find the killer?" Anna fiddled with the zipper of the backpack purse between her feet.

"Yes. But I'm afraid I haven't gotten very far." Cassie wished there was something she could tell Anna to offer hope.

"Do you have any suspects?"

Judd immediately popped into Cassie's mind. "Yes. But I don't know if it's going to pan out, so I don't really want to say who it is."

"I understand. But you believe me that Zach is innocent, right? Even though I wasn't there."

Cassie slowed down as she came up behind another car and turned to look at Anna. "Of course."

Anna smiled a bit more, but it still didn't reach her eyes. Cassie couldn't imagine coping with this mess at the same time as being pregnant. Anna's emotions must have been swirling.

A coffee shop appeared at the next curve in the highway. Cassie pointed. "Maybe we could stop and bring Zach a doughnut and a coffee."

"He probably needs it." Anna took her wallet out of her purse.

"My treat." Cassie pulled into the drive-thru and ordered two double-double coffees and an Earl Grey tea for herself. She bought a full box of doughnuts to leave with the officers, hoping to earn a bit of favour for Zach.

Ten minutes later, they pulled into the station. They entered the first foyer, and after explaining their intentions to visit Zach, a lady officer buzzed them through a secure door and led them down the hall to the rear of the building. She let Cassie keep one doughnut for Zach, checked the coffee, and after flashing a big smile at the girls, took the box with the remaining doughnuts back to the front with her.

A tall, brawny officer led them into a small room with a table and four chairs. He directed the girls to sit on the far side and closed the door behind him.

Anna set the coffees down and tapped the table with her fingernails.

"Take a deep breath." Cassie sipped her tea and rubbed Anna's back with her free hand.

Moments later, the door popped open, and Zach stepped in. The officer closed the door behind him and stood guard outside the room, the gun on his hip showing through the long, skinny window.

"Zachy!" Anna leapt to her feet and ran to him. He lifted his handcuffed arms over her head so he could hold her. She instantly melted into his embrace.

"Hey, baby." Zach kissed her gently.

"Do you mean me? Or do you mean the actual baby?" Anna smiled.

Zach threw a quick glance at Cassie.

"It's okay. I told her." Anna helped Zach lift his arms back over her head, and they took a seat beside each other, across from Cassie.

"I won't tell anyone," Cassie reassured him.

Anna tilted her head downward to avoid his gaze and lowered her voice. "I also told her the truth about where I was when you found Lloyd."

"Anna! What did you do that for?"

Cassie's cup sat on the table, and she wrapped both hands around it. "The truth is going to come out."

Zach rubbed his forehead. "I don't want you getting in trouble, too, babe." He grabbed Anna's hands with his cuffed ones.

"I only told Cassie, and I did so because she's trying to solve the case and get you out of here."

"You are?" Zach raised his eyebrows.

"I don't know how much I can do, but yes. Can you answer a few questions for me?"

"Of course!"

With Anna leaning on his shoulder, Zach spent the next few minutes going over everything that had happened. He reiterated how he'd caught the big fish, gone farther downstream to where it began to narrow, and seen a capsized aluminum boat sticking out of the cattail reeds by the shore.

When he went to investigate, he saw Lloyd, facedown in a couple of feet of water.

Without hesitation, he drove his boat as close as he could, jumped in the water, and waded through the weeds and mud. Lloyd's fishing pole floated beside him, its line snagged on a tree branch near the shore. Lloyd's feet were wrapped in weeds.

"And then I turned him over, and…" Zach shut his eyes and turned his head away from Anna. "It was horrible. I'd never seen a dead body before."

"I can't imagine." Cassie tried to think of the questions she saw the detectives ask in the BBC mystery shows she watched. "Did you see anything else out of the ordinary?"

"No. Maybe. It all happened so fast. I couldn't believe what I was seeing."

"Did he have a life jacket on?"

"Yes. But it wasn't zipped properly."

"What did you do next?"

"I swam back to the boat to grab my phone and call 911. The operator told me to stay put until the police boat came."

Cassie took another sip of tea. "What did you do in the time between the call and when the police came?"

"I went to get Anna." Zach's cheeks turned red. "I know I should've stayed right there, but she wasn't far and—"

"You don't have to explain." Cassie reached across the table and placed her hand on Zach's. "I probably would've done the same thing."

"And when the police arrived, I was there with Zach at the scene." Anna looped her arm in Zach's. "I didn't realize until after I gave my statement that they assumed I was there the whole time."

Cassie nodded. "Okay, you two. Think hard. Was there anyone else around? Did you see any other boats when you went to get Anna? Are there any other little details you can remember about anything? Even if you don't think it's significant."

Anna and Zach looked at each other and spent a few moments in silence. Finally, Anna shook her head, followed by Zach doing the same.

"I'm sorry, Cassie." Zach finally reached for his coffee cup. "I wish I could remember something else."

"It's okay. But if you do think of something, please let Anna know the next time you call." Cassie stood and nodded toward the door. "I'll see if he'll let you have a few minutes of privacy."

Zach reached out his cuffed hands to grasp Cassie's wrist as she walked by. "Thank you for trying to help. And for bringing Anna."

"Of course." Cassie smiled and knocked on the door. The officer let her out and held up his hand to Zach through the window, showing him he had five minutes left to visit.

"Are they really not going to investigate this case further?" Cassie leaned back against the wall opposite the officer.

"I can't discuss the details, ma'am."

"So, an innocent man just goes to jail?" Cassie waved her hand toward the room with Zach and Anna. She could feel her blood starting to get warm. This whole situation was beyond ridiculous.

"If he doesn't plead guilty, he'll have a trial, like everyone else."

"And what if they find him innocent?"

"Then the case will reopen. But..." He glanced down

the hall and then back at Cassie. "I don't think that will happen. The evidence speaks for itself."

"Argh!" Cassie pushed herself off the wall until she stood straight again. "But it doesn't! He didn't do it. There has to be more evidence to prove it."

The officer stared blankly at Cassie and then turned to open the door. "Time's up."

Cassie sighed and walked down the hallway to the front door with Anna. She resisted the urge to take back the box of doughnuts sitting on the reception counter as they passed. The lady officer merely smiled at them and buzzed them through to the foyer.

Back in the vehicle, Cassie and Anna drove in silence for a few minutes. It gave Cassie time to go over Zach's story. Nothing had really changed from the first version she'd heard, except that Anna wasn't there the first time Zach found the body. Technically, the evidence did point toward him, but Cassie knew there had to be something to prove someone else did it.

So what really happened? It had to be Judd. He was the only one with a motive and the opportunity. And for that matter, the strength.

"I need to think about something else." Anna's voice interrupted Cassie's thoughts. "Lexy told me you had a date with Daniel. How'd it go?"

"It wasn't a date." Cassie focussed on the road ahead of her. "I just showed him around town."

"Lexy said you'd say that." Anna grinned.

Cassie was glad to see her smile, even if it was at her

own expense. "Lexy's trying to cause trouble."

"Tell me about him. What's he like?"

"He seems like a nice guy." Cassie became distinctly aware her cheeks were becoming warm. "He likes books."

Anna laughed. "I see. What else? Where's he from again?"

"Toronto, I think."

"What did he do there?"

Cassie thought a moment. "I'm not sure."

"Oh." Anna turned to Cassie. "But he's single?"

"I assume so—not that it matters." Cassie shot her friend a sideways glance.

"Has he ever been married?"

"I'm not sure."

"Where did he get all the money to pay you a year up front?"

"I don't know. I'm not going to ask him." Cassie made a mental note to ask Lexy to keep her mouth shut.

"Then what do you know about him?" Anna chuckled.

"Not too much. Like I said, I was only showing him around."

But Anna raised a good question. What did she know about Daniel? He knew about her Grams, her mom, her town, and her passions. But what had he revealed to her about himself?

Cassie suddenly remembered the lack of information when she'd searched Daniel on the internet. And where did he get the money? She shook her head. No point jumping to conclusions. He probably sold a house or something.

She smiled as she recalled Daniel in the boat with her, going to see the sparrows that morning. She couldn't believe he'd never really spent time on the water. There! That was something she knew about him. He didn't even know how to dress for it. Cassie grinned again, thinking of Daniel's birding outfit and the silly boots.

"What's wrong?" Anna asked. "Why are you slowing down?"

"I, uh—" Cassie reaccelerated. "Nothing. I just remembered something."

Anna shrugged and took a sip of her coffee.

At least Cassie hoped it was nothing. But maybe it wasn't. If Daniel hadn't spent any time near the water and he was a big city boy, why did he have a pair of muddy rubber boots?

The possible answer frightened her.

She needed to find out more about him, immediately.

Chapter 15

Cassie waited next to the cash counter for Maggie to finish with her current customer. Pumpkin chirped from her napping spot on a stack of woven place mats. "Silly girl! You can't sleep there." Cassie picked her up and cradled her.

"Have a great day!" Maggie handed the customer a brown paper bag with the Olde Crow Primitives logo printed on the side.

"Oh! This is so cute!" The lady fingered the black-and-tan checked bow tied to the handle.

Cassie smiled as the customer exited. She loved hearing her customers enjoy the little touches she put into things. She scanned the room to see Grams serving two ladies at the wooden sign collection and five or six other customers roaming the store.

"How's it going in here?"

Maggie scratched Pumpkin's chin. "It's been steady, but we have it under control. Go. Do what you need to do to help Zach."

Cassie bit her lip and set the cat on the counter. "Are you sure? I mean—"

"I'm sure. Now get out of here so I can help these customers." Maggie winked.

"You're the best sister-in-law ever!" Cassie leaned in to give Maggie a quick hug and hurried to the back door. Pumpkin jumped off the counter with a thud and followed at Cassie's heels. She squeezed through the door behind her owner.

In the hall, Cassie paused. She looked up the stairs toward her apartment then at the door to Daniel's bookshop. She bit her lip again. What should she do first?

She already knew there wasn't any information about Daniel on the internet, so running upstairs to do research would be useless at this point. And she didn't want to pursue the leads on Judd any further until she dealt with the whole Daniel possibility.

Cassie stepped up to the bookshop door and held her hand to the knob. Why was Daniel so secretive? And how had she not seen it sooner? She took a deep breath, knocked once, and opened the door.

"Daniel? You here?" She crossed the threshold into The Book Nook. It was coming together nicely. A few crates of books lay scattered about on the floor, but the shelves were mostly full now.

"Hey, Cass! Come on in." Daniel popped his head out from behind a row of shelves.

She swallowed to try and moisten her dry throat.

"Meow!" Pumpkin offered her hello as she rubbed her

face against the corner of a crate.

"Yes, you can come in too." Daniel crouched and held his hand out, rubbing his fingers together for Pumpkin. The cat ignored him, moved on to the next crate, and sniffed it.

"It looks great in here." Cassie noticed a number of black-and-white photos hanging on the ends of each row of bookshelves. Some were of people, but most were of landscapes. They reminded her of Ansel Adams's style of photography. "These are nice."

"Thanks. How was Zach? Were you able to find out any other useful information?"

Cassie narrowed her eyes and studied Daniel as he pulled a few more books out of the box without taking his eyes off her. Why was he so interested in what she'd found out? Did he suspect she might be on to him?

"He's feeling pretty down. That happens when you go to jail for a crime you didn't commit," Cassie snapped, without meaning to.

Daniel furrowed his brow but returned to shelving books. "That's too bad. I hope you figure it out soon."

Cassie scooted around Daniel and plunked herself down in one of the comfy chairs. "What did you do before you decided to open this bookshop?" She twirled her hair with her finger and swallowed again.

Daniel avoided her gaze and stared into his crate of books. "Oh, you know. City job stuff."

"What kind of job?"

"I had a business." He stood and disappeared into one of the book aisles.

"What kind of business?" Cassie raised her voice so he would be sure to hear her. He was really going out of his way to avoid answering the question.

"Sales, mostly." He poked his head out again and gave her a charming smile. "Hey. I really enjoyed our walk by the river last night. Do you think we could do it again?"

Her stomach flipped when she recalled how close he'd held her after she'd tripped. It was hard to resist him, but Cassie put herself on guard. Why was he being so elusive? She should probably accept the offer for a walk. It might be a good way to get more information from him.

But, if he was somehow involved in Lloyd's death, did she want to spend more time alone with him? And even if he wasn't, did she want to give him the wrong idea? She didn't want to lead him on when she clearly didn't want a relationship with him. But wasn't it nice to spend time with him?

"I'll have to see," she finally managed to say. "I have a lot to do today." She stood and weaved her way through the maze of crates on the floor.

"Um. Okay." Daniel gently tossed the books in his hand into the crate and stepped out after her.

"Speaking of walking, I forgot to ask you why your boots were so muddy." It wasn't a smooth transition into the topic, but she couldn't think of anything else. She was certain the sleuths in her books only knew what to say because they had a writer behind their words.

Daniel raised an eyebrow. "My boots? Why?"

"Oh, I don't know. You said you hadn't been out to the

water yet, or for a walk, yet your boots were covered in mud."

"They're muddy because I watched my friends do the Mud Run in the city a couple of weeks ago. I took some pictures."

Cassie sighed and eyed him carefully. "Which Mud Run?"

Daniel ignored her question and stepped closer to her. "Cassie, are you all right? You're acting kind of strange."

"I'm fine. Sorry. Just busy and trying to figure out how to help Zach."

Daniel's eyes widened. "Are you questioning me as a suspect?"

Cassie felt her cheeks get warm. "No. Maybe. No—of course not! I have to run. C'mon, Pumpkin!" The cat followed her. "I'll talk to you later."

"Cassie—"

She shut the door and stood in the hallway. She closed her eyes and took a deep breath. That didn't go as planned. She started up the stairs but turned back to go into Olde Crow Primitives instead. Her purse was still behind the counter, and she wanted to take it with her to her apartment.

"Back so soon?" Maggie was wiping off the cash counter. Grams still talked to the ladies by the wooden sign display. She saw Cassie and gave a quick wave.

"Forgot my purse." Cassie reached below the counter to grab it when a delivery man in a brown uniform poked his head in the door.

"Do you know where I'd find D.J. Sawyer?" He looked

at the black console in his hand. "It lists this address."

"Daniel Sawyer? He's around the side at The Book Nook." Cassie pointed in that direction.

"Thanks." He nodded and left.

Cassie turned to see Maggie with her mouth dropped open. "What?"

"Did he say 'D.J. Sawyer'?"

"Yeah. It must be Daniel." Cassie threw her purse strap over her head to rest it on her shoulder.

"Daniel is D.J. Sawyer?"

"I guess so. Why?"

"You don't know who D.J. Sawyer is, do you?" Maggie's eyes opened wide with disbelief.

"Obviously not. Care to enlighten me?"

"He's a famous photographer from Toronto. He does black-and-white photos of renowned people from around the world." Maggie put her hand on her hip.

"What? He's famous?"

"No wonder he can afford to pay you a year up front." Maggie glanced toward the wall where Daniel's bookshop stood on the other side. "I wonder what he's doing with a bookshop in Banford?"

Cassie recalled the pictures in Daniel's store. Those must have been his photographs. He was famous? He knew famous people? How could he not have told her this? She thought of the conversation they'd just had about his previous job. Had he been mocking her the whole time?

"I've gotta go," Cassie announced and left the store even quicker than she came. Pumpkin bounded after her up the stairs and into her apartment. Moments later Cassie sat in her office, in front of her computer.

"D.J. Sawyer," Cassie spoke as she typed the words into the search engine.

Instantly, results filled her screen. She bypassed the web page results and clicked on Images. Daniel's face and photographs were everywhere. Daniel in a tux next to a celebrity. Daniel with his arm around a beautiful girl. Daniel shirtless, lying on a beach beside a different girl in a skimpy bikini. Black-and-white photos of landscapes, like those in the bookstore, and famous celebrities. Really famous celebrities.

Cassie clicked back to the article results as blood pumped through her veins. How could this be? Why did he keep this from her? No, why did he *lie* to her about all this? She felt like such a fool.

She dove into the articles.

The first one was about Daniel's recent breakup with some plastic model. She caught him cheating with her maid. Apparently, he'd cheated on her numerous times, but this one was the last straw. The article came complete with photos of Daniel with six other women. The same charming smile he'd given her not moments ago stared back at Cassie from the screen in front of her. Each time, his arm around someone else.

The screen blurred as Cassie's eyes filled with tears. How could she have been so stupid? Just when she thought she might be able to start trusting a man again, he managed to slap her in the face harder than she'd ever been hit before.

"Argh!" She pounded the desk with her fist. Pumpkin ran out of the room.

Even though this revelation about Daniel pretty much put him in the clear for Lloyd's murder, she almost wished it hadn't. It might be easier for her to take if he was a murderer, rather than the womanizing cheat he'd turned out to be.

Cassie stood and grabbed her purse from the kitchen. At least now she was back to one prime suspect—Judd.

And it was time to see for herself what was really growing in those fields.

Chapter 16

Cassie shoved the last bite of a doughnut into her mouth as she drove over the swing bridge. Judd wasn't the only one who could murder a doughnut. Drummond's Bakery had helped lift up her mood on more than one occasion. She only had to make sure it didn't become a regular habit.

As she drove out of town, the photos of Daniel with all the women danced their way through her mind. She wished she'd bought a second doughnut.

Instead, she fought off the images and tried to focus on Judd. He had to be the murderer. He was the only one left with means, motive, and opportunity. If she could find the marijuana plants and find proof that would link Judd to them, she could approach the police with a solid theory.

Cassie drove past the Hutchinses' driveway and continued on past a small forest. Right after, a farmer's lane cut through the edge of the field, walled by the trees on one side. A metal gate closed off the entrance, but Cassie pulled into the lane anyway and parked before the gate.

She hopped out of her vehicle and looked up and down the road. No one was around, so she approached the gate and looked at the latch. It was a twisted piece of wire. She quickly untwisted it and opened the gate. It squealed so loudly she heard a dog start barking in the distance. It was probably Judd's.

As quickly as she could, Cassie hopped in the SUV and drove past the gate. Then she leapt out of the vehicle, shut the gate again, and hopped back in.

She was glad she had an SUV, for the trail ahead was definitely meant for tractors only. She eased her way over the large potholes and around the larger rocks, while at the same time trying to get her vehicle out of sight of the road as quickly as possible.

Soon, the lane stopped. She was at the end of the first field, but another field lay between her and the river. To her right, the forest headed toward the Hutchinses', or rather Ross Sheffield's land, if this wasn't already part of it.

Cassie glanced at the river. If she wasn't mistaken, this was the field the Henslow's sparrows were nesting in! She hadn't realized how close the Hutchinses lived to the field, and therefore to the spot where Lloyd was murdered across the river. It would explain why Lloyd chose that spot to fish, and it also gave Judd a quick escape route.

She pulled the SUV into a small clearing behind a swath of cedar trees. Hopping out, Cassie grabbed her binoculars, phone, and a camera with a zoom lens.

Ironically, Daniel's photography skills could have come in handy that afternoon. She frowned at the thought of him and resisted the urge to slam the door.

She glanced back at the river. Should she head there and make her way by shore? She shook her head at herself. She didn't want to disturb the sparrows, and she knew from being in the boat that no marijuana grew along the shore.

Cassie gathered her courage and headed into the cedar forest in the direction of the Hutchinses' house. If something really was planted out there, she'd end up walking right through it.

A mosquito landed on her neck, and she gave it a swat. She grimaced as she realized she'd forgotten bug spray and waved her hand around her head to ward off the critters. Ahead of her, cedar trees grew in thick clusters, making it impossible to see through them to anything beyond. The winding route she'd have to take to get around them could easily set her off course.

Maybe it wouldn't be so easy to find the plants.

Cassie rounded another group of trees and noticed the forest already thinning. Aspens and poplars grew tall, mixed in with the cedars. She paused to raise her binoculars and check out a beautiful red-and-black scarlet tanager as it called to her from the top of a poplar.

The bird's red plumage glowed like fire as the sunlight hit it. Birds never failed to amaze her. A breeze blew across her face, and she smiled. Until she smelled the skunk.

Cassie quickly lowered her binoculars and scanned the forest around her. She didn't see a skunk, but that didn't mean one wasn't hiding nearby. The thick cedar branches made it impossible to tell. She carefully stepped farther into the forest and wove her way around a few more clusters and through a patch of aspens.

The skunk smelled stronger, but she had to take her chances. This was the direction she needed to go. As she eased her way around the next group of cedars, she was startled by the source of the smell.

She giggled quietly to herself. It wasn't a skunk! It was marijuana plants.

A lot of marijuana plants.

The four-foot plants had long, skinny leaves, with jagged edges. Cassie was surprised at how big the plants were, and it was only early summer. They were planted in sporadic spots among a mixture of five-foot trees. She figured that must hide them better from view from any low-flying aircraft than if they were planted in rows.

The smell became stronger as Cassie edged her way around the edge of the grow area. She rubbed her nose and avoided taking deep breaths. At the far end of the garden, Cassie untangled her binocular and camera straps and took off the camera's lens cap. She snapped a few photos and sighed.

How would this help her connect Judd to the plants? So there were pot plants there. It didn't make him guilty. She'd have to find something else.

Cassie was about to step out into the plants when a flash of blue caught her eye. She darted behind a group of cedars and ducked.

Someone was there.

She parted the branches in front of her, giving her a

view into the dark interior of the cedar cluster, but she could see nothing beyond. Slowly, she duck-walked around the trees, careful to hold her camera and binoculars apart so they didn't clunk together.

The spot of blue moved.

It was Judd.

He wore a blue-and-black checked, sleeveless flannel. A faded, black cap shaded his face from the sun.

Cassie's heart pounded. Is this what it was like to be a detective? Her stomach turned. This didn't feel fun and adventurous like in the cozy mystery books she read or the mystery shows she watched. Her stomach churned. What if he caught her? Would he hurt her? If he'd murdered his dad, he wouldn't hesitate to come after her.

And there she was, all alone with him in the back forty. This spot was much more private than the creek where Lloyd had been found. Cassie gulped.

She was there because Anna, Zach, Bubba, and Ida needed her to be.

After saying a quick prayer for safety, Cassie snapped a couple of photos. She lowered her camera to check the LCD screen. None of the photos captured Judd's face. She looked around. There wasn't really another spot nearby where she could stay hidden, but she also needed a better view of Judd.

Another duck-walk step forward, and Cassie raised her camera. This time, she held it higher, above her head. She clicked the shutter and quickly dropped the camera down. Not only did she miss Judd's face, she missed his body all together.

A slicing noise caught her attention. Judd was taking pruning shears to the tops and ends of the plants, his back to her.

Cassie decided to take the chance and lunge over to a lone cedar at the edge of the garden. She had to really hunch to stay hidden behind the small tree. She mentally reminded herself not to wear a light-pink shirt next time she needed to be stealthy.

After a couple of moments, Cassie decided Judd hadn't seen her movement. She carefully turned herself around while staying low in the same spot. She peeked around the tree. Judd now faced her direction.

The slicing of the pruning shears covered the noise of the camera shutter as Cassie snapped a few more pictures. This time when she checked the LCD screen, she could clearly see Judd's face. She smiled at her accomplishment. Not only was Judd pictured with the marijuana, but he was working it. There would be no questioning that this was his crop.

Cassie peeked around the tree. Judd faced the other way again. She wanted a few more pictures for good measure but decided against it. She already had the evidence she needed. Now she'd have to get it to Officer Welby.

Judd turned again, so Cassie hunched back down. He worked on the next couple of plants and slowly headed in her direction. She'd have to get out of there soon. Could she risk another lunge?

She held her binoculars and camera apart again and waited for Judd to turn.

Her pocket buzzed and vibrated.

Her phone!

Her stomach sank. She'd forgotten to turn it off.

Cassie fumbled in her pocket and hit the button to stop the buzzing. The scissoring sound of Judd's pruning shears stopped.

She risked a quick peek around the tree. Judd walked toward her, the shears hanging open at his side. Cassie gulped and ducked behind the tree again, resisting the urge to panic.

Now what?

She pivoted on her foot and felt her heel hit something. A pinecone was wedged underneath her shoe. She whipped it down the side of the field, and it hit a tree trunk with a small *thunk*.

Cassie took another peek. Judd turned his head toward the noise and changed his direction. Taking her chance, she lunged to the tree cluster, resuming her original hiding place.

Judd was still walking away.

Remaining crouched, she let out a sigh of relief. The pinecone had worked, but clearly, it was time to leave. She took another breath to gain courage when a cold hand grabbed her shoulder from behind.

"Hold it right there."

Chapter 17

Cassie whipped around and swung her fist through the air, hoping to connect with whoever was behind her.

The intruder caught her arm by the wrist and, with his other hand, raised a finger to his lips to instruct her to be quiet.

It was Officer Welby.

He used two fingers to point at his eyes, and then one to point at Judd.

He'd been watching the whole time.

Cassie let out a relieved sigh and relaxed her shoulders. She showed him the camera screen and the photo she had of Judd and the marijuana.

Officer Welby gave her a thumbs up, and motioned with his hands for her to stay put. He hunched down and stepped into the garden with his hand on the gun holster at his side.

Cassie waited a few moments, and then followed him, keeping a safe distance.

Judd stood at the edge of the garden, looking into the trees on the far side. Officer Welby approached him from behind.

"Stay right where you are, Judd."

Judd whipped around, armed with his pruning shears.

"Drop them." Officer Welby kept his hand ready at his holster. "Don't make this difficult."

Thunk. The shears pierced the ground and Judd raised his hands.

"Quite the little grow-op you got here."

"It ain't mine." Judd spat on the ground.

Officer Welby glanced at the pruning shears and then returned his gaze to Judd. "Really. Just pruning the cedars then?"

"I'm allowed to grow it. Law's changed in Canada."

"You're allowed to grow four plants. I'd say you have four hundred here. Is that about right?"

Judd shrugged. "What's she doing here?" He nodded toward Cassie.

"What?" Officer Welby turned around. "I thought I told you to stay put."

Taking advantage of the distraction, Judd spun around and took off into the woods.

"Great," Officer Welby muttered and took off after Judd. "Judd! I have a gun. I'm ordering you to stop!"

Judd darted around a group of trees with Officer Welby at his heels. Cassie followed the sound of thrashing branches and heavy footfalls as best as she could, holding her camera and binoculars.

"Stop, Judd!" Officer Welby's voice rang through the forest.

Cassie darted around a wall of cedars to find herself in the field behind the Hutchinses' house.

Judd continued to run through the long grass, Officer Welby at his heels.

She raised her camera and grabbed a couple of quick shots of the pursuit.

Moments later, Officer Welby leapt through the air and landed on Judd, pulling him to the ground.

"I told you to stop!"

"I ain't done nothing wrong!"

Cassie finally caught up to the pair. She snapped a few more pictures of Officer Welby with his knee in Judd's back, slapping handcuffs onto Judd's wrists.

"Put that away," he ordered Cassie as he pulled Judd to his feet. "And you—march!"

Judd scowled as he tromped his way through the long grass. When they reached the Hutchinses' yard, Officer Welby stooped to brush off his pants.

"Ma!" Judd yelled. "Ma, come out here!"

"Judd Hutchins." Officer Welby tugged on Judd's handcuffs. "I'm placing you under arrest for illegal activities surrounding the growth of marijuana."

"What's goin' on?" The wooden screen door slammed shut behind Gladys. "What'd ya do, Judd?"

"Ma! He's taking me in for—"

"Quiet!" Officer Welby ordered as he pulled a small card from his pocket. "I need to read you your rights."

"The marijuana in the field is Judd's, Gladys." Cassie kept her tone gentle.

"And you!" Officer Welby glared at her. "I can charge you with trespassing and interfering in police business!"

"Me? You want to charge me for doing your job?" Cassie huffed.

"I was doing my job just fine. And I could have avoided that traipse through the woods if it wasn't for you."

"I'm talking about the murder. Isn't that why you're here?"

"Murder?" Judd gasped. "I didn't murder no one!"

"What are you talking about, Miss Bridgestone?" Officer Welby yanked on Judd's cuffs. "I'm here on a tip from Ross Sheffield about Judd growing pot on his land."

Cassie put her hand on her hip. "I know Zach didn't do it. But you refuse to listen to reason. Judd, on the other hand, has means, motive, and opportunity."

"How dare you?" Gladys snapped.

"You recently took out a large life insurance policy on Lloyd, didn't you?"

"So what?"

Officer Welby tilted his head toward Gladys. "You did?"

Cassie turned to Judd. "And you need a lot of money to get your auto shop started."

"I wasn't taking no money from my ma. My money is sitting in that field back there."

"You stupid boy!" Gladys rushed to Judd and slapped his arm. "I just lost your pa, and now you gonna get yourself locked up and leave me too!"

"Would the marijuana have provided all the money you needed?" Cassie pressed. "Or did you need the life insurance to top up your bank account?"

"All right, I've heard enough." Officer Welby tugged on Judd and led him toward the police cruiser. "Time to get you booked."

"But what about the murder?" Cassie asked. "You're at least going to look into it, right?"

"I didn't murder Pa!" Judd yelled.

"Oh, Judd!" Gladys started to cry as she followed behind.

"It wasn't me." Judd looked at his mother. "I was at work that morning."

"I know you didn't." Gladys rubbed the side of Judd's arm. "I just wish you wouldn't have gotten yourself in this other mess. Especially right now."

"Sorry, Ma." Judd ducked his head as Officer Welby guided him into the back seat of the police cruiser.

"Wait." Cassie put her hand on the door before Officer Welby could shut it. "You said you were at work?"

Judd nodded.

"That's enough, Miss Bridgestone." Officer Welby slammed the door shut despite Cassie's resistance. "And I'll need to take your camera as evidence."

"My camera?" Cassie frowned. "Can't I send you the photos? Or give you the memory card?"

He held out his hand.

Cassie sighed and pulled the strap over her head,

hesitating for a second before she placed the camera in the officer's hand.

He gave her a smug smile. "Thanks. Your cooperation will be noted while I review the pending charges against you."

Cassie frowned as Officer Welby hopped in the front seat and drove down the driveway, lights unnecessarily flashing on the roof of the car.

Gladys sobbed. Cassie turned to face her and put her hand on the woman's arm, but Gladys immediately wrenched her arm free.

"You get out of here."

"Gladys. I—"

"Now." She pointed down the driveway.

Cassie decided it best not to argue and headed off.

She'd forgotten how long the Hutchinses' driveway was. She had a bit of a hike ahead of her, now that she had to go back to the road first, past the forest, and then all the way down the farmer's lane on foot.

Tears welled up, but she pushed them back. Did Judd really have an alibi? If he didn't do it, then who was left? Would Officer Welby really charge her for interfering? She shook her head to answer her own thought. Surely he was bluffing and throwing his weight around? Those photos she took provided all the evidence he needed to charge Judd— both for the illegal grow-op and for resisting arrest.

Cassie reached the end of the driveway and turned onto the road. She took a deep breath to try and calm her racing mind. She smiled as a wood thrush hopped into a tree beside the ditch. Lifting her binoculars, she admired his proud, spotted chest before he skittered away into the woods again. Cassie uttered a small prayer of thanks. God knew how much birds calmed her—how their beauty stirred her soul.

A red-tailed hawk soared overhead. A warm, comforting feeling surged through her body. Even in the midst of the chaos, Cassie felt peace. God was with her. He was in control. She had to remember that.

And then she remembered something else. People who murder are also liars. Just because Judd said he was at work didn't mean he actually was.

She picked up the pace as she turned down the farmer's lane to retrieve her SUV. Her next stop was obvious.

She needed to visit Brown's Garage.

Chapter 18

Gravel crunched underneath the tires as Cassie pulled her SUV into the lot at Brown's Garage. The clock on the dashboard blinked as it turned to six o'clock.

Cassie smiled at the perfect timing. She waited in the vehicle while two mechanics closed the big overhead doors and exited the front with their lunch coolers.

When they pulled out of the lot, she hopped out of her vehicle, approached the garage, and peered through the greasy window.

Mr. Brown stood behind the reception counter, doing paperwork, his glasses low on his nose. His thin, graying hair clung to the sides of his head.

She gave a quick knock and stepped inside.

"Cassie. Nice to see you."

"Hi, Mr. Brown."

"The air conditioning still working okay?"

"Yes. No problems there." She shoved her hands in the pockets of her jean shorts.

Mr. Brown peered over the top of his glasses. "How can I help you? We're closed until Monday now. Is it something urgent?"

"Uh, no. My vehicle's fine." Cassie chewed the corner of her cheek, trying to find the words without being obvious.

"I'm here about Judd Hutchins, actually."

Mr. Brown clicked his tongue. "Awful business, about Lloyd."

"Ah, yeah. And it gets worse."

"How so?"

"Officer Welby just arrested Judd for growing marijuana."

"Oh no." Mr. Brown rubbed his forehead. "And so soon after Lloyd's death."

Cassie swallowed to combat her dry throat. "I know, right? Were you here when he received the news about his dad?"

Mr. Brown nodded. "It was horrible. We had our heads stuck under a car on the hoist, working on a nasty transmission that morning. Then Officer Welby came in to deliver the news. Judd didn't take it well."

"Oh. You were with him all morning under the car?"

"Yeah. It was a rotten job. Why?"

Cassie shrugged. "Just wondering. Good to know he was with someone when he found out, that's all."

"Yeah. I thought I was going to have to drive him home. He was pretty shaken up."

"Did he, uh, act strangely at all before that? Did he go

anywhere or arrive late for work?"

Mr. Brown furrowed his brows. "No, as I said, we were working on the transmission. He actually got here early, because he knew the job was on the schedule and it would take a long time."

Cassie still wasn't convinced. If Lloyd's time of death was around eight, Judd could have had time to get home, change out of wet clothes, and head to the shop by nine.

"So, Judd was here slightly before nine?"

"Nine? No, he was here at seven thirty."

Cassie's stomach sank. If that were true, then he had a solid alibi. "That early?"

"Yup. He's been working a lot of extra hours lately. Making extra money and learning as much as possible about the different jobs so he can be ready when he opens his own shop."

"You know about that?"

"Of course." Mr. Brown nodded. "I'm the one who encouraged him in the first place. There's enough repair work to go around. Hate to lose a good mechanic though." He rubbed the back of his neck. "Looks like it's happened anyway."

Cassie nodded. "Awful nice of you to try and help him out like that, though."

"He's a good lad. A bit rough around the edges, but he does good work." He tilted his head a bit. "What was it you wanted again?"

"To let you know about the arrest."

Mr. Brown furrowed his brows. "Oh, okay. Thanks."

"Bye." Cassie avoided Mr. Brown's curious gaze and let herself out. At this point, Cassie didn't care if he believed her or not. She had the information she needed. Only, it wasn't the information she wanted. Not that she wanted Judd to be a murderer, but someone other than Zach needed to be.

She returned to her vehicle and drove the quick jaunt across the swing bridge to her building. As she pulled past the bookshop and into the parking lot, she caught a quick glimpse of Daniel looking out and smiling.

Her stomach turned, and it wasn't from a lack of food. A doughnut may have provided comfort earlier in the day, but the last thing she wanted now was to eat. How could she? Cassie shut the engine off and gripped the steering wheel. She lowered her forehead onto it. What had she done? Judd and Gladys had just lost their loved one. And now, because of her, he was off to jail, and Gladys had to deal with Cassie accusing her son of murder.

All she needed on top of this debacle was Daniel trying to add her to his list of conquests. She snatched her purse and binoculars from the passenger seat and climbed out of the vehicle. If she walked fast enough, maybe he wouldn't see her go by the store.

Fat chance. As she rounded the corner, he stood outside his storefront, waiting for her.

"Cassie! Hi!" He flashed his charming smile. The same one he sported in all the pictures, with all the different women.

"Hi." She kept walking. "Sorry. Can't talk. Gotta run!"

He wrinkled his nose and grabbed her arm as she walked by, forcing her to stop. "Hey. Hold up. Why do you smell like skunk?"

"Let go of me." She pulled her arm back.

He instantly released his grip. "I'm sorry. Are you okay?" His eyes softened, and he tilted his head with genuine concern. At least it looked genuine. But then, so did his charming smile.

"I'm fine," she lied. "I have a lot to do."

"So, I guess there's no time for a walk tonight?"

"No."

"Maybe tomorrow then." He flashed his teeth at her again.

She blinked. "I'm not sure. It's a busy week." Soft wrinkles appeared around saddened eyes, but she shrugged it off. It wasn't her fault he was a Casanova. She wasn't going to be his next victim.

"Did I do something to offend you?" He reached forward to touch her arm but then dropped his hand at the last second.

Cassie sighed as she took a step closer to the door leading to the stairwell. "I know who you are, D.J. Sawyer."

Daniel closed his eyes. "How'd you find out?"

"Did you think I was some ignorant hick? Thought you could pull one over on me?"

"Cassie, no!" Daniel shook his head. "It's not like that at all."

"I know exactly what it's like. Daniel Sawyer might not be online, but D.J. Sawyer certainly is."

"Oh no." He covered his face with his hand and rubbed his forehead.

"Oh no, you got caught? Or oh no, I won't be your next conquest?"

"No. No!" He glared at her. "I thought you knew me better than that."

"Know you? I don't know you at all. I don't know anything about you." Cassie jabbed her finger toward him. Her binoculars swung out from her arm and came back and hit her in the hip. She winced but ignored the pain. "You flashed your playboy smile at me and thought I'd fall under your spell! Well, guess what? I may be a country girl, but I'm a smart girl. And…"

Cassie stopped. She wasn't smart. Not at all. She'd hurt Gladys, gotten Judd put in jail, failed to help Zach, and fallen for a playboy.

Yes. She had to admit it—she'd fallen for Daniel. But now, that was over.

She turned on her heel toward the door and fumbled in her purse for the key.

Daniel stepped up behind her. "I never thought you were stupid. But I guess if you believe everything you read in the media, you're not as smart as I thought, either."

Cassie continued to dig for her key as she heard Daniel's footfalls move away from her, followed by the slam of The Book Nook door.

By the time she found the key, her eyes were too blurred with tears to find the lock. She fumbled around with the key for a few seconds until it slipped into the hole. She yanked the door open and ran up the stairs to her apartment.

"Meow!" Pumpkin greeted her as Cassie burst through the door.

Cassie had never been so grateful to see her. She put her purse and binoculars onto the counter and scooped Pumpkin into her arms. The cat purred.

A glance over her shoulder showed a full cat food dish. Maggie must have topped it up when she brought Pumpkin upstairs, after the store closed.

She squeezed the kitty tight, straggled into the living room, and dropped onto the sofa. Her favourite afghan sat on the arm of the couch. She lifted Pumpkin so she could drape it over her lap and set the cat back down. Pumpkin snuggled close and kneaded the blanket.

The tears flowed. These last few days had been a complete disaster.

"Oh, God!" she cried but didn't know how to proceed with the rest of the prayer. She was a complete failure. She'd failed to help Zach, and now he was going to jail. Anna would be pregnant and alone. She'd broke her promise to Ida. She'd made things worse for a newly widowed woman. Not only did someone murder Gladys's husband, but her son got taken away too.

What a mess! And to top it off, she'd failed herself. She'd allowed herself to feel things for Daniel she wasn't supposed to feel. And he'd had the nerve to imply she was dumb for believing the media. Pictures don't lie.

Her sorrow was her own fault, though. She knew he wasn't a believer. What else could she expect from someone in his position who didn't have a relationship with God? She'd set herself up to get hurt by entertaining thoughts about him in the first place. She deserved what she got. There was a reason she guarded herself and refused to trust men, at least as far as her love life was concerned. She'd broken her own rules, and now she was forced to reap the consequences.

Cassie's thoughts turned to Zach again. He was alone, in a cold cell, and he was counting on her to help him. What was she going to tell Anna?

The mystery book she was reading sat on the end table. She couldn't even bring herself to pick it up. She knew any efforts to focus would be futile. Instead, she threw on some pajamas, ignoring the rest of her usual nighttime routine, and crawled into bed.

Even well after Cassie had tucked herself in, the thoughts continued to whirl about in her mind, darting among the Hutchins family, Zach and Anna, and Daniel. They played like a carousel, round and round in her mind for hours, until she finally dozed off.

Chapter 19

"It's not your fault Judd's in jail. It's his!" Grams smeared butter on her toast and glanced across the table at Cassie. "He's the one who broke the law."

Cassie pushed the eggs on her plate with her fork. She'd woken up feeling so low she'd almost cancelled her pre-church breakfast date with Grams. "I guess."

"There's no guessing about it. It's a consequence of his own behaviour."

The Hardcastle Restaurant and Pub was usually one of Cassie's favourite places to be. Its relaxed atmosphere and British feel calmed her and made her feel like she was in England. Old beams crisscrossed on the low ceiling, and the wooden wainscoting, bar, and booths were all painted black. Old lanterns provided dim mood lighting, and the rest of the light came through the paned windows, accented by the flower boxes outside.

She sighed. "I just feel bad he was taken from Gladys so soon after she lost Lloyd. That *is* my fault. If I hadn't told

Ross Sheffield about the marijuana—"

"Stop it, Cassie." Grams put her butter knife down and stared at her granddaughter. "You thought the pot belonged to Ross, remember? You didn't tell him on purpose. Ross, on the other hand, knew what he was doing when he told the cops about Judd. He chose to do it so soon after Lloyd's death. Not you."

Cassie nodded and took a sip of her Earl Grey tea. "You're right."

"Of course I'm right." Grams took a bite of bacon and winked at Cassie. "Now let's deal with the next issue."

"What next issue?"

"The fact you feel guilty for not solving the murder yet."

Cassie groaned and leaned back against the wooden booth. "How did you know?"

"Because my granddaughter is loving and compassionate, like her mother, Sandra, was." Grams patted Cassie's hand. "And I know you well. You take other people's burdens to heart so much they become your own. It's a gift from God, but you have to keep your eyes on Him to get through it."

"I promised them I would find the real murderer."

"And there's still time. You might feel like you're at a dead end, but the truth is still out there. You're a smart cookie. Don't give up."

Cassie sat tall again and picked up a piece of toast. "Thanks, Grams."

"And since we're on a roll, let's deal with the third thing."

"What third thing?" Cassie avoided Grams's gaze by smearing jam on her toast.

"That bookshop boy."

"Ugh." Cassie's shoulders slumped. "Can I not get anything by you?"

Grams chuckled. "You should know better. Let's talk about it."

"There's nothing to say. He's a playboy, and he tried to play me."

"Go deeper."

Cassie sighed. "I was stupid and started to fall for him. There. I said it. And yes, before you remind me—I know. I need to find someone who loves God more than me, and me more—"

"Than himself. Yet you fell for him anyway."

"I tried not to. But from the moment I met him, my heart... reacted. I should know better than to let myself trust so easily. I'm not ready yet."

Grams gently tapped the table. "And there it is."

"What do you mean?"

"Why aren't you ready yet, Cassie? It's been three and a half years since you broke it off with Chris."

"Please don't say his name." Cassie toyed with the handle on her teacup.

"Chris."

"What are you doing?"

"Helping you. Why does it hurt to hear his name?"

"Why are you dragging this back up?" Cassie leaned against the booth.

"To help you. Why does it hurt?"

"You know why!"

"Tell me."

Cassie bent forward and whispered across the table. "Because he cheated on me a month before our wedding. There! I said it. Happy?"

"I'll never be happy about that, dear." Grams patted Cassie's hand again. "And neither should you. But you do need to forgive him."

Cassie sighed and closed her eyes. "I can't."

"Maybe not in your own strength, but with God's, you can."

"And then what?"

"And then you heal. And let God direct you to the man of His choosing, not yours."

Cassie nodded and fought tears. "I knew from the beginning I shouldn't have been with him. But I ignored God's promptings and pursued him anyway."

"Sometimes we learn things the hard way." Grams gave Cassie's hand a squeeze. "Now eat up."

Cassie stared at the remaining eggs and bacon on her plate. Even though she hadn't eaten the night before, she still didn't have much of an appetite. All the same, she forced herself to take a bite of the bacon and washed it down with a sip of tea.

The waitress passed by on her way to deliver a breakfast plate to the next booth. She popped her head in on the return trip. "Everything good here, ladies?"

"Excellent." Grams beamed and scooped up a forkful

of eggs. She turned to her granddaughter. "Tell me about the evidence."

Cassie let out a deep breath. "Unfortunately, what we have points to Zach. It doesn't look good for him. And there's even more evidence the police don't know about yet."

"How so?"

"Anna wasn't actually with him when he first found the body. She was checking out the sparrow nest site."

"Uh-oh."

"It gets worse." Cassie leaned forward so Grams could hear her as she spoke softly. "It's not only the wedding Zach and Anna need money for. Anna's pregnant."

"Oh dear." Grams touched the side of her cheek with her palm.

"So, the motive for Zach stealing a big fish from Lloyd, to win the tournament, stands strong." Cassie frowned. "Add in his two previous assault charges and Anna lying about being at the scene and—"

"It doesn't look good."

Cassie shook her head. "Nope."

"But there's still a lot of speculation involved. What are the facts? What else have you found out?"

Cassie paused to collect the roaming thoughts in her mind. "Gladys and Lloyd took out large life insurance policies a few weeks ago. She said it was because their daughter insisted. Something about one of her in-laws dying and not providing for the other."

"Plausible." Grams nodded.

"Yet Gladys and Lloyd were being evicted from their house by Ross Sheffield. Their rent was really low, and they'd need a lot of money to live elsewhere. And Judd is looking to open his own auto mechanic shop, so he needs money too."

Grams continued to nod. "Hence the pot growing."

"Yes. But Judd seems to have a solid alibi, and Gladys couldn't have physically performed the deed herself."

"Right."

"As you mentioned, originally I thought the pot belonged to Ross Sheffield. The Hutchinses were dragging out the eviction as long as they could, so I thought he killed Lloyd to get them out of the house quicker so he could expand his crops. But it turned out he only wants to grow soybeans."

"Reason enough to evict but not to murder." Grams poured more hot water into her teacup.

"Right. And he has an alibi, anyway. Unless his secretary is lying. But why would she?"

"Maybe she's in on it?"

"Even if she was, it brings us back to motive. Why kill over a crop of soybeans, especially since it's already past their planting date?"

Grams rubbed her chin. "So, what are we missing?"

"I wish I knew."

"Anything else odd happen lately?"

Cassie thought for a moment. "The morning before the murder, Anna and I were out in one of Bubba's small boats, checking out the nest site. Eric and Marjorie sped by in his boat so quickly he almost capsized us."

"That horrid little man." Grams's eyes narrowed, and she speared a piece of egg with her fork. "How does that relate to the murder?"

"I don't know if it does. It was the only other thing I could think of."

"So, you're back at square one?"

Cassie nodded. "Square one! Of course. That's what I can do." She pushed the button on her phone to check the time. "After church, I'll head out to the crime scene. If I have to start over again, I'll start at the beginning."

"That's my girl." Grams set her utensils on her empty plate and pushed it forward. "I knew you wouldn't give up. Let me pray for you before we go to church."

Cassie gently placed her hands into Grams's outstretched palms and bowed her head. Nope. She wasn't giving up.

The truth was out there, and she was more determined than ever to find it.

Chapter 20

Cassie returned her church dress to her closet and pulled on a pair of army-green cargo shorts and a black tee. Pumpkin hopped onto the bed. Cassie plunked down beside the big orange-and-white cat and scratched her behind the ears. The cat purred and fell over, exposing her plump belly.

A quick glance at her phone showed there were only about ten minutes before Lexy was due to arrive. At church, Cassie had filled Lexy in on the plan to return to the crime scene, and she'd insisted on coming with her.

Cassie was grateful. She didn't want to go out on the water alone and have too much time to think—especially since Pastor John's sermon had been about forgiveness. She wondered if Grams had put him up to it. He had some excellent points, though, and Cassie knew it was time to address the bitterness.

She'd met Chris during her last year of college. He'd doted on her and told her how wonderful and beautiful she was. After two dates, she was completely head over heels, even though a prompting in her heart told her to beware. She ignored it and ignored it even further when she decided to stay in the city and move in with Chris.

Grams was disappointed, but Cassie hadn't cared. She'd wanted love. Ever since her mother had died when Cassie was eighteen, she'd felt a gaping hole in her heart. She longed to feel the unconditional love her mother had given her. And even though God was the one who needed to fill that void, she'd tried to fill it with Chris instead.

The problem was that Chris had a hole in his heart too. Only he decided he needed more than one woman to fill his. The cheating had started in their second year together, but Cassie had dismissed the evidence and believed his lies.

It happened again their third year, but she couldn't prove it. Instead, he'd taken the opportunity to pledge his love for her by proposing in a romantic setting on a beach in Ottawa. It was nighttime, and there was a full moon. He'd placed lit tiki torches in the sand around a blanket. He'd brought champagne and strawberries, and the diamond glistened in the moonlight. Cassie had thought it was the best night of her life.

A few months later, four weeks before their wedding, Cassie came home from work early and found Chris in their apartment with his co-worker, Barbara.

There was no more denying anything.

Despite Chris's efforts to smooth things over with his magic words, the spell he'd had over Cassie had finally been broken. Within two days, she'd left the city and moved in with Grams back in Banford. Grams had nursed Cassie's broken heart for the next few months.

Cassie passed the time by working at Grams's store, Olde Crow Primitives. It turned out the timing was perfect, as Grams had been praying for a way to retire. She'd struck a good deal with Cassie for low monthly payments and a good sale price for the building. It was the best decision Cassie could have made.

She loved being back in Banford and appreciated the small-town charm even more after living in the city for a while. Her business degree came in handy, and the pieces of her life finally started to come back together.

And, despite the efforts of a few local bachelors, she stayed happily single.

Except she wasn't happy being single. She just couldn't bring herself to trust anyone else. And now, when she dared to open her heart a little, Daniel smashed it all over again.

But that was her own fault. Like Chris, Daniel wasn't a Christian. In that sense, Cassie was kind of glad she'd found out what he was like ahead of time. No need to repeat the patterns of her past.

One thing she'd learned from her experience with Chris, and from Grams, and from her mother's wonderful marriage with her father, was that God needed to be at the center of a marriage. And even then, it didn't mean it would be easy.

Her eyes suddenly opened to the truth. She'd needed to find those photos of Daniel. She had been letting her heart slip, even though her head had told her not to. It was the kick in the pants she'd required to get him out of her mind.

Pumpkin sat up, shook her head, and scratched at her ear. That was her signal to Cassie that she'd had enough petting.

Cassie rose from the bed and continued to get ready. She slipped on a pair of loose lace-up shoes and grabbed her binoculars. Her camera would've been handy, but Officer Welby still had it in his possession. Her phone camera would have to do. She shoved it in her pocket as the door popped open and Lexy walked in.

"Hi! Ready?" Her brown ponytail swung through the air as she leaned in for a hug. She had on a pair of denim shorts with a green tank top that highlighted her eyes.

"Yup! Let's go."

Lexy eyed the binoculars in Cassie's hands. "Are you going to make me stop and look at birds?"

"Not for long. We're going right by there, anyway. Besides, binoculars are handy to have."

Lexy rolled her eyes and laughed as they headed out the door.

On the short walk to Bubba's, Cassie filled Lexy in on the news about Daniel's identity. It wasn't something she'd wanted to bring up earlier in a church foyer full of people.

"D.J. Sawyer?" Lexy narrowed her eyes. "I think I may have heard of him."

"I guess I live under a rock."

"But it's a nice rock." Lexy elbowed Cassie in jest.

They turned down the sidewalk to Bubba's and within moments, passed though the shop and climbed into the boat. Cassie pulled the cord, and the engine roared to life.

Lexy leaned back on her elbows to bask in the sun and let the water spray onto her face.

Cassie sped the boat down the river and then crossed to the other side to make a quick stop in front of the sparrow field. All was quiet.

Since it was almost noon, Cassie didn't expect any different but couldn't resist the urge to check. She started the boat again and steered it back to the other side of the river and into the small channel where Lloyd had been found.

She slowed her speed. "Eyes open." She nudged Lexy with her foot.

"I'm working on my tan." Lexy sat up and looked around. "What are we looking for?"

"I have no idea."

"Do you even know where the body was?"

"I called Anna after church. She gave me a pretty good description." Cassie pointed. "We need to look for the three big weeping willow trees on the east bank."

"She didn't want to come?"

"Ida is taking her to see Zach. I don't think she was too keen on coming back here, anyway."

The girls scanned the water as Cassie slowly moved the boat down the creek. Nothing seemed out of the ordinary. The water had slight ripples from the breeze, and the cattails stood tall on the banks.

The odd red-winged blackbird sang from the top of a stalk, and a pair of mallards poked in and out of the weeds ahead.

"There are the willows." Lexy pointed to three, large willows leaning over the creek with long branches of leaves teasing the top of the water.

Cassie knocked the engine down to a crawl and eased into the reeds. Then she slapped her palm to her forehead. "I forgot to bring hip waders."

"I guess you're going to get wet then." Lexy giggled.

"You mean, *we* are going to get wet."

"Nuh-uh. I only volunteered to come as company." Lexy's smile stretched from ear to ear.

"Thanks!" Cassie pulled the boat closer to shore, careful not to get the motor caught up in the weeds, and dropped anchor.

The girls silently stared at a section of broken cattail stalks and stirred up weeds.

"That must be where it happened." Lexy's smile disappeared.

Cassie's stomach turned. "How awful. Poor Lloyd." She pulled her phone out of her pocket and tucked it into her bra. Then she kicked off her shoes and stretched her leg over the side of the boat. "Use the oar to keep the boat steady."

Lexy's eyes widened. "You're really going in?" She grabbed the oar, jabbed it into the shallow water until it stuck in the ground underneath, then pushed on it for leverage to keep the boat upright as Cassie eased her other leg over the side and jumped in.

She gave Lexy a satisfied grin. "Yup!" The water lapped at the bottom of her shorts.

"Yuck." Lexy wrinkled her nose. "How does that mud feel?"

"Moisturizing. You should try it!"

"Just don't start sinking. I'm not coming in to get you."

Cassie giggled and waded carefully toward the broken reeds.

The giggles faded. How awful it was to be standing where someone had killed Lloyd. She studied the cattails. There was no way to tell if they were broken by the murderer, the overturned boat, the police officers, or by Lloyd himself before the fact. Nothing else seemed unusual. Some algae and other weeds had been disturbed by the crime scene, and Cassie pushed them away from her bare leg, but to no avail.

"Anything?" Lexy asked, still hanging on to the oar.

"No." Cassie sighed. "I'm going to walk to shore."

She waded through about forty feet of cattails and weedy water, until she came out onto a pebbly shore. She winced as a sharp rock dug into the sole of her foot.

The willow trees loomed overhead. The grass was about knee-high, and hints of former landscaping poked through by means of unkempt bushes and peonies in the distance. Someone must have lived on that piece of land, many years ago.

Cassie pushed aside some hanging willow branches and walked underneath one of the trees. The branches were so full and bushy, she couldn't even see Lexy anymore.

"Anything?" Lexy hollered.

"No! I'm going to keep walking a bit." Cassie pushed

more branches away and made her way under the second tree.

Under this canopy, a faded, yellow rope was tied to the trunk of the tree. The end led off into the water. Cassie examined the trunk. There were no markings or rubbings from the rope, so it couldn't have been there very long. She pulled her phone out of her bra and snapped some photos.

"I found a rope," she called to Lexy.

"And?"

"I don't know yet." She put her phone back in her bra and tracked the rope to where it disappeared into the river. Wading back into the water, Cassie put hand over hand and followed it, taking extra care not to tug on it and change its position. The hanging willow branches and thick cattails made the task difficult, but she managed to push her way though.

She emerged on the other side of the willow and continued until she was about knee-deep in the water. The cattail stalks were broken in several places where the rope lay underwater. She pushed some stalks aside so she could see Lexy.

"Can you row this way?"

"I can try."

Cassie heard the splash of the paddle in the water as she kept on following the rope until water reached the bottom of her shorts again.

"What's it attached to?" Lexy asked, as she neared Cassie with the boat.

"I'm not sure. But it feels light." And then the end of

the rope appeared in Cassie's hand. It was roughly severed, and weeds were caught up in the frayed end. "I guess that answers your question."

"Is it significant?"

Cassie held the end of the rope and surveyed the distance between where she stood and where Lloyd had been murdered. It was only about twenty feet away. "I don't know. Maybe."

Lexy jabbed the oar into the ground again, to steady the boat while Cassie leaned over the side and pushed off the ground with her feet to get the momentum needed to climb back in. She rolled into the bottom of the boat, her legs covered in green slime.

"Oh, that's gross." Lexy wrinkled her nose.

Cassie scooped some of the algae off her legs and slapped some on Lexy's shin with a smirk.

"You're going to pay for that!" Lexy shook her leg and quickly wiped off the grime, trying not to touch it. She quickly reached over the side of the boat to rinse her hand. "You're trapped in here with me, you know!"

"Wait! That's it!" Cassie bolted upright onto the bench seat. "That's what the rope led to!"

"You lost me."

"A trap. Someone must have had a trap, or a fish cage, hidden here, stocked and ready for the tournament!"

"You mean with big fish already in it?" Lexy asked.

"Yes. And poor Lloyd must have stumbled across it and got caught by the cheaters."

"Would that be enough to kill him over?"

"First prize is thirty thousand dollars, a boat, and a trailer. You tell me. People have killed for less." Cassie rubbed her chin.

"And Zach came along not long after it happened."

"Of course!" Cassie raised both hands in the air. "That's why he caught a big fish down here. It must have escaped from the trap during all the kerfuffle!"

"It does make sense." Lexy nodded. "So how do we prove it? What's our next move?"

"For starters, we head back to Bubba's and find out who's in second place after Zach."

"You mean the next biggest fish?"

"Yes. If you remember, Bubba keeps the results secret until the winners are announced at the closing barbecue tonight. If they think they've won, they'll be waiting to collect their prize."

"And you'll be waiting to catch them."

"Exactly." Cassie pulled the cord to start the motor and zoomed down the river to Bubba's Bait Shop.

Chapter 21

Cassie tied the boat to the dock and held it steady while Lexy climbed out. Then she snapped up her binoculars and the boat key and hopped out too.

"Are you going to call Officer Welby?" Lexy smoothed her ponytail as they traipsed up the dock.

"Not yet. Let's find out who has the second-biggest fish first."

Lexy nodded as the girls approached the large, metal fish tank behind the bait shop that held the fish tournament entries.

Cassie peered over the edge at the large bass swimming back and forth in the tank. There were certainly some big fish in there. Which one would lead them to the murderer?

Following Lexy into the shop, Cassie found Bubba leaning over the live bait tanks, scooping out some minnows into a pail for a customer.

"Bubba. I really need to talk to you."

"Hey, Cassie. What's up?" He dumped one more fish

into the pail and set it on the ground.

Cassie leaned in close and whispered, "I might have a lead, but I need your help."

Bubba tapped the net handle on the side of the tank to remove excess water. "Okay, give me a second." He pulled the lid back across the bait tank and brought the pail to the cash counter.

Four customers puttered around the shop, all in their fishing garb. What if Cassie stood in the same room as the murderer right now? It could be one of them. Or any of the other 196 tournament participants.

She frowned and checked her phone.

The tournament ended in two and a half hours. The entrants would be arriving soon to weigh in their last catches of the weekend.

Bubba finished with his customer and headed their way. "How can I help?"

"Can we go out back?" Cassie nodded toward the employee door.

"Anna?" Bubba called.

She popped her head out of the little office in the corner. "Yeah? Oh! Hey, Cassie. Hey, Lexy."

Cassie and Lexy waved their hellos.

"I'm going out back for a sec. Mind the store?"

"Sure." Anna nodded. Her smile was weak.

Cassie walked over and gave her friend a quick hug. "Spirits up. I'm doing everything I can to help Zach."

Anna gave an extra squeeze before releasing the hug and heading over to the cash counter to help the next customer.

Bubba held the door open for the girls to exit before him and followed them out behind the shop. "What's going on?"

"We just came from the crime scene." Cassie kept her voice low. "I found a rope tied to a tree on the shore, so I followed it out into the water. It ended not far from where Lloyd's body was. The end was frayed, like something had been cut off."

"A fish cage." Bubba's eyes widened.

"That's exactly what we thought." Cassie glanced at Lexy.

"So, what are you thinking?" Bubba bumped his ball cap while giving his forehead a scratch.

"That someone killed Lloyd because he caught them cheating."

"And that's why Zach caught such a big fish near there," Lexy added.

Bubba straightened his ball cap. "Makes sense."

"Where's your list?" Cassie pointed at the fish tank. "Who has the next biggest fish after Zach?"

His face paled.

"What is it?" Lexy placed her hand on Bubba's forearm.

"Eric and Marjorie. They're next in line."

Cassie's eyes narrowed.

"Who?" Lexy asked.

"The jerks who almost capsized me and Anna." Cassie put her hand on her hip. "Why am I not surprised?"

"Oh, them." Lexy frowned. "Should we call the cops now?"

Cassie shook her head. "Not yet. We need to find more evidence."

"He uses this boat launch." Bubba pointed through the fence to the ramp next door. "His truck and trailer will be parked nearby."

Cassie smiled. "What's it look like?"

"You can't miss it. It's a junky yellow truck with black roll bars."

"Thanks, Bubba. Stick these in your office for me?" Cassie handed him her binoculars. "Let's go, Lexy."

The girls left the shop and raced down to the boat launch parking lot.

"Do you see it?" Cassie used her hand to shield her eyes from the sun. The parking lot wasn't very big.

"It's not here." Lexy shook her head.

"Let's try the street." They jogged up the hill.

The street was lined on both sides with trucks and empty boat trailers. Cassie scanned the opposite side, looking one way and then the other.

No yellow truck.

She waited for a car to pass and crossed, looking at the row of trucks and trailers on the other side.

"There!" Cassie pointed. "Up by the church!"

She jogged back across the street to meet Lexy, and together they kept pace up the sidewalk toward the old stone United Church on the corner—and Eric's truck.

"What are we looking for?" Lexy leaned over and put her hands on her knees to catch her breath.

"I don't know. The fish cage?" Cassie pulled back a tarp

covering stuff in the bed of the pickup. "Here. Help me hold this."

Lexy grabbed the edge of the tarp while Cassie rummaged through the junk underneath. There was an old tire, fishing tackle, a broken rod, and a few dented toolboxes. Behind the toolboxes, two large paint pails sat pushed up against the cab of the truck.

"These look promising." Cassie leaned far over the edge of the truck to grab the edge of the first pail and pull it toward her. A bunch of rusty nails rattled around in the bottom. "Or not."

She pulled on the top of the second pail. More nails.

They replaced the tarp and tried the other side of the truck, only to be disappointed by more of the same useless junk.

"What about inside?" Lexy nodded toward the truck door.

Cassie took a deep breath and pulled the handle. It was locked. "Now I'm even more suspicious. Who locks their vehicle in Banford?"

"No one, unless they have something to hide." Lexy put her hands on her hips. "What about the passenger side?"

The girls walked back to the sidewalk and tried the passenger door. Locked.

But the window was open a couple of inches.

"Will your arm fit through there?" Cassie grabbed Lexy's bony wrist.

"Oh, sure. Make me the criminal."

"Of course!" Cassie grinned.

Lexy slid her hand through the crack but couldn't push through past her forearm.

"Hang on." Cassie lifted the tarp again and grabbed the broken rod, a chisel, and a hammer.

"What are you going to do? Break the window?" Lexy stood back.

"Watch." Cassie used the chisel to snap off a length of fishing line from the rod. Then she tied the hammer to the end of the line and slid it through the window crack. She stuck her fingers through the opening and balanced the line on the end of them as she swung the hammer back and forth toward the lock button.

"Smarty pants." Lexy grinned.

After about ten tries, the hammer connected, and the lock clicked. "It worked!"

Lexy threw the rod and the tools back into the truck bed while Cassie climbed into the cab and looked around. She wrinkled her nose at the smell of cigarette smoke and sweat.

A few fast-food wrappers and drink bottles littered the floor. Junk filled the console between the two seats.

She threw two empty bottles on the floor with the rest and rummaged through the newspapers, fishing lures, cigarette packs, and sunglasses. A few receipts stuck out of a closed compartment in the console. Cassie popped it open and pulled them out. Maybe one of them would show the purchase of a fish cage, or a container that could double as one.

The first few receipts were for gasoline. Then there was

one for an oil filter and oil. Another receipt for a fast-food order.

"Find anything?" Lexy rested her hand on the top of the door and leaned in.

"Not yet."

"Hey! What are you doing?" A male voice shouted from down the street.

Lexy grasped Cassie's leg. "A man is running up the sidewalk."

Cassie looked out the back of the cab window, but the grime and the stuff in the bed blocked her view. She returned the receipts to the compartment, slammed it shut, and jumped out of the truck.

It was Eric.

"Oh, hi, Eric." Cassie waved as he reached them. "Is this your truck?"

"What do you think you're doing?" he snarled.

Cassie shrugged. "Your lights were on. I was just shutting them off."

Eric narrowed his eyes and stared at her. "The doors were locked."

"Not this one. It was open."

Eric pushed Cassie aside and leaned into the cab. "You better not have stolen somethin'."

"Not at all." Cassie held her hands up so he could see they were empty. Lexy followed suit. "Just trying to be helpful. I hope your truck starts okay."

Eric glared at the girls as he slammed the truck door and walked around the other side.

"That was quick thinking." Lexy joined Cassie as she walked back to Bubba's.

"I saw it in a show once." Cassie smirked, then let the smirk fade. "Unfortunately, we're no further ahead with evidence."

"Now what?"

"Oh!" Cassie picked up the pace. "Maybe we can catch Marjorie before Eric gets that trailer turned around! He'll have to drive around the block."

The girls jogged to Bubba's and down the boat ramp. Marjorie sat in the boat, holding it alongside the dock, awaiting Eric's return with the trailer.

"Hey, Marjorie!" Cassie slowed her pace and walked out onto the dock. "How was the fishing today?"

"Not bad." Marjorie eyed the girls before turning her sights back to the street.

"I heard you caught a big fish this weekend!" Cassie stood above the boat, looking down in it for any signs of a cage.

"Yup. Eric got a whopper."

"That's great! Do you think it's big enough to win the tournament?" Lexy rubbed the end of her ponytail between her fingers.

"Pretty sure."

"Where did you catch it?" Cassie asked.

"Why?"

"Just curious. I heard stories of a lot of big fish coming out of the creek over there this year." Cassie pointed down the river.

"That creek? Nah." Marjorie shrugged. "Nothing but a lot of young bass in there. We always fish the other end of the canal, through the locks." She pointed in the opposite direction.

"Really?" Cassie tilted her head. "Because I saw you down by the creek on Wednesday morning. In fact, you almost capsized my boat."

Marjorie laughed. "That was you?"

"Yes, it was." Cassie felt her face get warm but took a breath to calm her anger. "So, clearly, you were down by the creek."

"Not fishin'. Joyridin'."

Cassie's heart sank. Was that true? Did they really catch their fish far away from the creek? If so, her theory about the fish cage was completely off. But maybe she was lying to remove suspicion about her and Eric being anywhere near Lloyd.

Eric's yellow truck pulled into the lot.

"I think you're lying," Cassie sputtered. They clearly weren't going to confess on their own, so confrontation it was.

"What the heck are you talking about?" Marjorie shook her head and rolled her eyes.

"What are you doing, Cass?" Lexy nudged her friend's arm.

Eric backed the trailer down the ramp and into the water. Marjorie fired up the motor and expertly steered the boat onto the trailer on her first attempt.

Cassie ran back up the dock and over to Eric as he

hopped out of the truck.

"You did it, didn't you?" Cassie yelled at Eric. "You used a stocked fish cage to cheat!"

Eric's face turned red. He breathed out so forcefully through his nostrils that they flared, and he gave a bit of a snort. "You better watch what you're saying, missy!" He waved a finger at her. "Don't you dare be accusing me of cheatin'!"

"I'm accusing you of a lot more than cheating!"

"Like what, exactly?" Eric took a step closer to Cassie.

"Take it easy, you two!" Bubba came out of the store, followed by two customers.

"Murder. That's what! Lloyd Hutchins caught you with your cage, and you had to silence him!"

"Murder? You've got a lot of nerve!"

Cassie stepped forward and pointed her finger in his face. "Yes. I do. But not as much as you. How could you do that to poor Lloyd?"

Marjorie joined the argument. "I already told you we caught the fish past the locks."

"So you say." Cassie flipped her hair behind her shoulder.

"They did." One of the customers with Bubba spoke up. "I was nearby when they caught it. I saw him reel it in on his line. They were hootin' and hollerin'."

"See?" Marjorie raised a hand in the air to make her point stronger.

Cassie stepped back.

"Get out of here." Eric waved his hand at Cassie.

"Dumb girl. We should've capsized you," Marjorie muttered.

"C'mon, Cassie." Bubba coaxed her to follow him to the shop.

But Cassie stood motionless. Heat rose to her cheeks but not from anger. What had she done? Had she not learned her lesson from the encounter with Judd and Gladys? But she was convinced Eric and Marjorie were guilty.

Yet they weren't. And she'd made a complete fool of herself. And disrespected them. Was this how a Christian was supposed to act?

And what about the murder?

Time had run out.

Chapter 22

Cassie waved at Lexy as she drove off. She let out a big sigh. All she wanted to do right then was take a shower and cuddle with Pumpkin for a bit before heading out to the fishing tournament's closing barbecue. She had completely humiliated herself and angered Eric and Marjorie.

She hoped she could muster up enough courage to apologize to them at the barbecue.

This detective stuff wasn't as easy as it seemed to be in books and movies, and she certainly wasn't a natural Nancy Drew.

Cassie rounded the corner of the building and popped the key out from underneath her phone case, where she kept it when she didn't carry her purse. When she stepped into the stairwell, Daniel burst into the hallway from the bookshop.

"Cassie!" He leapt in front of her.

"Not now, please." Cassie tried to brush by him and head up the stairs.

"Please wait." He stood his ground, not allowing her to pass.

She crossed her arms and pursed her lips. "What is it?"

"I've, uh… finished the shop. Want to come see?"

"Not right now. I need to take a shower."

Daniel looked at the dried green slime on Cassie's legs. "What happened?"

"Never mind. Let me by, please."

"Please, Cassie. I want to talk to you. Can you come in for just a minute? You look like you could use a tea. I stocked up on Earl Grey…" He stepped out of the way, but held his arm out toward the bookshop door.

Cassie took a step up the stairs.

"Please?" He replaced his usual charming smile with a pained stare.

She sighed and stepped back down. "Five minutes." She might as well get it over with. The day couldn't get any worse.

Daniel held the bookstore door open with his arm so Cassie could enter before him. Her jaw dropped as she crossed the threshold.

It was beautiful. The crates had disappeared from the floor, and in their place stood three wooden tables in the centre aisle, with books exhibited on small, tiered displays. The wooden shelves were stocked full, complimented on the ends by the famous black-and-white photos of D.J. Sawyer.

At the far end, throw pillows adorned the comfy chairs, and more photos lined the fireplace mantel. The old windows all held book displays, except for the one with the small coffee bar.

Daniel approached the coffee machine, popped in an Earl Grey pod, and picked out a mug with a cat on it for Cassie. "What do you think?"

"It's really nice. Perfect for this town."

"Thanks." He stood silently, waiting for the tea to finish pouring. Then he handed the cup to Cassie and grabbed his own cup of coffee from the counter.

He must have seen her coming and already poured his, she figured, looking out into the parking lot through the window above the coffee bar. "What did you want to talk to me about?"

Daniel led her to the comfy chairs and let her pick the one she wanted to sit in, before settling into the one next to her. "First, I wanted to apologize."

"For what?" Cassie could think of a hundred things. She only wanted him to specify which one.

"For trying to hide who I was. For not being truthful with you from the beginning."

"Ha! So, you *were* hiding it."

"Of course I was. I'm not used to small towns. And you... You're—"

"Dumb?" Cassie raised an eyebrow.

"No. Not at all. The exact opposite, actually. You're one of the most intelligent women I've met in a long time."

She refused to be flattered. "That can't be hard. I saw the pictures of the bimbos you were hanging around with." The insult rolled off her tongue too easily.

Now who was being judgemental?

"Cassie, please."

She relented and took a sip of her tea.

"Those women, what you saw—it's not really like that." He set his coffee cup on the table, folded his hands together, and stared at them. "I'm not a playboy. Not at all. But because of my fame, and partly my manager, the media tried to portray me as someone I wasn't."

"I saw the pictures. There were all kinds of women. That wasn't faked."

"But it wasn't real, either. Most of those pictures were taken at gallery openings or parties I needed to attend for publicity. I just stood with them for the photo op. Nothing more."

"And the girl in the skimpy bikini on the beach?" Cassie wasn't going to let him pull one over on her.

"My cousin, Natalie." His eyes met hers. "It was a family reunion, but they cut everyone else out of the picture. If you look closely, you'll see nothing sensual about any of those photos."

Cassie studied his face. He held her gaze.

"And the model girlfriend you cheated on?"

Daniel closed his eyes and swallowed. "Half true. I had the model girlfriend, but she cheated on me. Not the other way around."

Cassie sat more upright. Could that be true? "Oh."

"We met at a dinner hosted by my manager. He thought it would be good for me to actually date one of the beautiful women for real." Daniel shifted in his chair. "Except it wasn't real. It was all for show. We went out in public for a number of months, until we really fell for each other. When I caught her with my manager, I realized *I* was the only one who really fell. She was playing along for the public image."

"I'm sorry." Cassie took another sip of tea and studied the tense lines in Daniel's face. He dropped his head and rubbed the back of his neck. It had to be hard for him, opening up to her like this.

Despite her cultivated inclination not to trust, something told her he was telling the truth.

"I was tired of the spotlight—and the lies." Daniel looked at her again. His eyes held unshed tears. "I had to get away. My parents live in Ottawa now, so I thought it would be a good idea to open a bookstore in a small town up this way, where I could be close to them. I figured I could display a few of my photos and live a less public life."

"If you wanted to get away from the lies, why did you lie to me?" Cassie wasn't quite ready to let him off the hook yet.

"I didn't lie. I just didn't completely fill you in." Daniel picked up his coffee cup again. "I was afraid if you knew who I really was, you'd find all the articles and think I was like they portrayed me in the media. And yet it happened anyway." He glanced at Cassie.

"You're right. I'm sorry."

"I guess I… I wanted someone to get to know the real me." He touched her knee. "I wanted *you* to know the real me."

Cassie held her mug with both hands and stared into it.

"Do you think we could start again?" Daniel took her mug and set it on the table. He grabbed her hand in his own. "I promise I'll be more open with you. Perhaps we could start with dinner?"

Cassie pulled her hand away and leaned back in her chair. "I think I need to be totally honest with you too."

He put his elbows on his knees and continued to lean forward. "Okay."

"I'm sorry if I misled you, but I'm not looking for any relationship with you beyond a landlord and tenant friendship." Her heart sank in her chest as she uttered the words.

"Oh." Daniel sat up. "I thought... I thought we hit it off well. I guess I was wrong."

"You weren't wrong. But you have to understand, my faith is the center of my life. I can't be with someone, in a deep relationship, without him sharing the same faith."

"I respect your faith, Cassie. I do. I would never step in the way of that. I'll even go to church with you."

Cassie shook her head. "I appreciate that, but it's not enough. I need to be with someone who is also a Christian. I want to worship with them and pray with them. To let them be the spiritual head of our relationship—the leader."

Daniel hung his head.

"I'm sorry. I hope you understand."

"I do. And I respect your loyalty to your beliefs. But I don't have to like it." He gave her a weak smile.

Cassie rose. "Now, I need to shower."

Daniel walked her to the door leading to the stairwell

and opened it for her. "Are you going to tell me why you're so filthy?"

"Nope!" She grinned. "I can still have some secrets."

"Now I'm pretty sure I don't want to know." He gave her arm a quick squeeze. "Thanks for listening."

Cassie nodded and headed to the stairs. So the media had lied after all. She shook her head, kicking herself for not knowing better. At least it had been resolved quickly and she was able to have the heart-to-heart with Daniel. Now he knew where she stood.

As usual, Pumpkin trotted into the room with her meowy greeting as Cassie entered the apartment. Cassie kicked off her shoes, and Pumpkin immediately sniffed them. Within a few moments, she was rolling all over them.

"I bet you like the river smell, eh?" Cassie scratched Pumpkin's head.

The conversation with Daniel replayed in her mind. She felt sad but also at peace. It was a strange feeling. Ultimately, she knew her actions had pleased God—at least she'd done something right that day.

And then it hit her. In telling Daniel she couldn't be with anyone who wasn't a believer, she had completely given over her relationships to God.

He was in charge of her love life now. She'd thought He was before, but now she could see the difference. She trusted Him above all else.

Cassie grabbed a glass and filled it with water. Leaning against the counter, she sipped from the goblet and allowed herself to think of Chris. The hurt remained, but the incident suddenly seemed to be way in her past. And something else was different.

The anger was gone.

A wave of peace flooded through her soul as she realized she'd finally forgiven Chris. It didn't excuse his behaviour, but it no longer had a hold over her.

Everything was truly in God's hands. She was no longer running from a relationship, if it was the one of His choosing. She could trust again, when the timing and the person were right. If it happened soon, she could embrace it. If she were meant to wait a few more years, she could handle that too. The point was, she had conceded control to her Creator.

Cassie let out a deep sigh of relief as Pumpkin wound around her ankles.

Maybe the day hadn't been a total loss, after all.

Chapter 23

After a refreshing shower, Cassie put on a pair of beige capris and a red, short-sleeved blouse. A perfect outfit for the barbecue. Flipping her damp hair upside down, she gave her curls another scrunch and then dried her hands on the fluffy towel she'd left on the bathroom counter. She chucked the towel into the overflowing laundry hamper and sighed as she stared at the mound of clothes. Generally, she avoided doing laundry on Sundays. It was her only day off, and she wanted to respect the day as one for rest and worship.

Cassie hit the button to wake up her phone.

Only three thirty.

She had plenty of time to run a load before the barbecue. She picked up an escaped sock, balanced the hamper against her hip, and opened her apartment door.

The door swung shut before Pumpkin had her chance to sneak out into the hall and follow. She meowed and scratched at the door.

"I'll be right back, silly." Cassie swung the hamper around to carry it with two hands.

She stepped into the laundry room. The washers were empty, so she chose her favourite and dumped the clothes in. Colours, whites, and towels were freely mixed together. Years ago, in college, Cassie discovered it didn't really make a difference whether she sorted her clothes or not, as long as she kept her expensive tops separate and washed any new, coloured clothes separately the first time. It was such a time saver to not have to sort clothes.

As she poured the detergent in the machine, her mind shifted to Lloyd and mulled over the mystery. She'd been so certain the frayed rope had been for a fish cage, but Eric and Marjorie weren't fishing near the area, and witnesses saw them catch their fish. How could she have been so wrong?

She thought about the time. The tournament officially ended at three thirty. For the next two hours, the remaining fishermen would be lined up at Bubba's to get their fish weighed. Would the real murderer be among them?

Cassie shoved the detergent and fabric softener bottles into her cupboard and carried the hamper to her apartment. When she opened the door, Pumpkin darted out.

"Hey! C'mere, you." Cassie set the hamper by the door and tried to grab Pumpkin. The cat escaped her grasp and ran up the stairs to the third floor.

"Pumpkin! Come!"

If cats could laugh, Pumpkin would be doing so. She crouched low on the top step and wagged her tail high, challenging Cassie.

But there was no way Cassie could be angry at her cat. Pumpkin was super cute, and it wasn't very often she got in this playful, chase-me mood.

Cassie slowly climbed the stairs, playfully stalking her kitty. Pumpkin continued to stare at her with wide eyes. She flattened her ears, lifted her rump slightly, and shook it, as if ready to pounce. Cassie took a few more steps up.

Pumpkin suddenly turned her head and twitched her nose a few times. Before Cassie could grab her, the cat jumped up the last step and ran to the rental door at the far end of the hall. It was open a crack, so she pushed her way in.

"Pumpkin! No!" Cassie ran to the door. The latch was broken and sometimes let loose if the door wasn't locked. She had to get it fixed, and soon. She pushed the door open a bit more. "Hello? Jake? Mitch?" No one answered.

Cassie wrinkled her nose at the distinct smell of body odor and fish. She'd have to air out the apartment after the guys left.

The open layout was a duplicate of her apartment below, but it certainly didn't look the same. Empty food containers covered the kitchen table, clothes hung on the backs of the chairs, and beyond that, some more clothes were strewn about on the back of the sofa.

Pumpkin rolled around on the ground beside the sofa, pushing herself up against a couple of empty, stacked, laundry baskets.

"That's where they are." Cassie recognized the two blue baskets as the ones that had gone missing from her laundry room a few days ago. She picked up Pumpkin. "C'mon, turkey."

She set her down again. What was on the basket? She fingered bits of green slime stuck to one of the sides. Then she noticed broken pieces of zip ties fastened around the edges of both baskets.

The blood drained from Cassie's head, and her throat went dry. Could it be?

She pulled her phone from her back pocket. Scrolling through her contacts, she stopped when she found the number for Bubba's Bait Shop. She chewed her fingernail as she waited for someone to answer.

"Bubba's Bait Shop. Can I help you?" Anna's voice sang through the phone.

"Anna! It's Cassie. I need to talk to Bubba right away."

"Oh, hey, Cassie. He's doing a bunch of weigh-ins right now. Can I have him call you back?"

"No. It has to do with the murder. I need to talk to him immediately."

"Hang on."

Cassie chewed through two fingernails and started on a third. "C'mon, Bubba!"

Pumpkin continued to sniff the baskets and rub up against them.

"What do you need, Cassie?" He finally came on the line.

"Hi! Do you have your weigh-in list on you?"

"Yup. I got it right here."

"Who is in third place?" Cassie's heart beat faster as she

heard papers rustling on Bubba's end of the line.

"Got it. Oh, yeah—those two new guys."

"Who?"

"Jake Thorpe and Mitch Miller."

Cassie felt like she was going to throw up.

"You still there?" Bubba asked.

"Yeah. I'm here." She swallowed. "Thanks. I'll be in touch, soon." The phone beeped as Bubba ended the call. Cassie shoved her phone in her pocket and steadied herself by gripping the edge of the sofa.

Jake and Mitch used the laundry baskets as a fish cage.

That could only mean…

They murdered Lloyd!

She shook her head. There was no way she was going to jump to conclusions again.

Yet the evidence was right there in front of her.

Upon closer examination, she noticed a small piece of frayed, yellow rope tied to the other end of one of the baskets.

She had to take pictures of this. She reached toward her back pocket.

"Hey! What are you doing?" Mitch burst through the door, holding a fishing rod and a tackle box. Jake appeared right behind him.

"Hi, guys!" Cassie tried to stop her voice from shaking. "Sorry to bother you. I was just looking for the baskets from the laundry room. Mind if I take them? I'm running short."

"Yes, I mind." Mitch closed the door with his foot, dropped his fishing equipment, and tromped toward her. He seemed bigger than Cassie remembered.

"Ease up, Mitch." Jake set his stuff down and held his hand up in a calming motion.

"She knows," Mitch replied.

Cassie skirted around to the other side of the sofa. "I know what? That you have my baskets? It's okay. You can keep them longer if you like."

"You think I'm stupid?" Mitch raised his voice and balled his fists.

"Mitch!" Jake hollered.

"I'm telling you, she knows. She was poking around at the bait shop earlier, talking about a fish cage and accusing someone else."

Cassie sidestepped around the sofa, trying to keep it between her and Mitch. "You must be mistaken." Her voice quivered. "That wasn't me."

As Mitch rounded the other end of the sofa, she made a dash toward the apartment door.

"Grab her!" Mitch shouted.

Jake caught Cassie's arm on her way by and yanked her back from the door. She tried wrestling out of his grip, but he was too strong.

"Help!" Cassie screamed.

"Be quiet, or I'll break your arm!" He tightened his grip as he wrenched her arm behind her back.

She winced. "What are you going to do?" She eyed Pumpkin, crouching beside the sofa. Cassie guessed she'd be hiding under it, if she could fit. Not a bad idea.

"Good question." Jake walked her farther into the

apartment. "Bring me that chair." He nodded at a kitchen chair, full of clothing.

Mitch tilted the chair to dump everything off and dragged it to the living room area. He pushed the coffee table against the sofa to make an open space.

Jake forced Cassie to sit in the chair. "Grab me some zip ties."

Mitch fetched his tackle box and plunked it down on the kitchen table, flattening a pizza box as he did so. "This is way out of hand, Mitch." He opened it and pulled out the ties. "You gonna kill her too?"

Jake pushed down on Cassie's shoulders to hold her in place. "I don't know!" His voice was rough and angry. "Let's hold her here for now and go claim our prize, first."

"Ha!" Cassie spewed out. "That's what you think." She instantly regretted saying that. How would it help her situation if they knew they weren't going to be the winners?

"Rowr!" Pumpkin jumped on top of the sofa.

"Get that thing out of here." Jake waved a hand at the cat.

"Don't hurt her!" Cassie begged.

Mitch handed Jake the zip ties and picked up the cat with two hands. Cassie bit her lip and fought back tears. He held the cat away from him, walked to the apartment door, and opened it to throw Pumpkin in the hall. Cassie sighed in relief.

"Here. Hold her while I tie these." Jake continued to push on Cassie's shoulder with one hand, while the ends of the long zip ties bounced up and down in the other.

Cassie took advantage of the opportunity and dove forward out of the chair and out of Jake's reach. She scurried to her feet and grabbed a half-full fast-food drink from the counter. Running toward the door, she threw the cup at Mitch, hoping to distract him enough to get away.

The cup hit Mitch in the chest, spraying pop all over the front of his shirt. Even so, he lunged forward and grabbed Cassie's wrist as she reached for the doorknob. "Think you're smart, do you?" He twisted Cassie's arm again.

"Ow!" Sharp pain shot through her shoulder and tears filled her eyes.

Mitch returned her to the chair, where Jake stood waiting with the zip ties.

Cassie let out a sob. She had found the murderers, but no one would ever find out.

Chapter 24

Mitch pushed on Cassie's wrists, holding them on the arms of the chair, while Jake wrapped a zip tie around her left foot and the chair leg.

He held her leg with such force, she couldn't even kick to resist. Instead, she flailed her right leg around, managing to connect with his arm.

"Stop it!" Jake growled and knelt on her right foot to hold it down while he pulled the zip tie tight.

"You won't get away with this." Cassie squirmed in the chair. "I'm not the only one who knows what you did."

Jake pulled the zip tie to secure her right ankle to the chair leg. "Sure. I bet the cops are on their way right now."

"It's true! Check my phone. I made a call to Bubba's Bait Shop not ten minutes ago." She leaned forward so Mitch could grab the phone from her back pocket. "He knows everything."

Mitch's Adam's apple bobbed up and down as he shot a wary glance at Jake.

"Check it." Jake fastened a zip tie around Cassie's left arm.

Mitch pulled the phone out of Cassie's pocket and swiped the screen. "No password?"

She shook her head.

He jabbed at it with his fat, dirty finger.

Jake secured Cassie's other wrist to the chair arm and stood. "Let me see that." He snatched the phone from Mitch's hands and stared at it. He gave the screen a few swipes. His face paled, and he threw the phone to the floor and grabbed Mitch's shirt collar. "Grab your stuff. We gotta go."

"What about her?" Mitch smoothed his shirt once Jake let go.

"We'll take her with us for insurance."

Not the decision Cassie had hoped for. If only she'd kept her mouth shut, they might have just gone to the barbecue, and she'd have had time to get free. Now, her time was up.

She tugged at the zip ties, but they dug into her skin. Jake and Mitch scurried around the apartment, throwing their clothes into a bag and grabbing the odds and ends they'd left scattered around the room.

Jake ducked into the bathroom and Mitch into the bedroom. Cassie hopped and inched the chair toward the door. A scratching noise caught her attention, and she heard a faint meow.

"Pumpkin!" she whispered as she scooted the chair across the floor.

Someone knocked on the door. "Cassie? You in there?"

"Daniel!" she screamed. "Help!"

The door flew open. Pumpkin bounded into the room, with Daniel at her heels.

"Cassie!" As he rushed toward her, Mitch and Jake ran back into the room.

"They murdered Lloyd!" she yelled.

"Argh!" Jake lunged toward Daniel and attacked him with a football tackle.

"Oof!" Caught by surprise, Daniel flew back against the wall then slid to the floor with Jake on top of him.

Jake pulled his arm back, ready to throw a punch, when Pumpkin jumped on his back, hissed, and dug her nails in.

"Get that wretched thing off of me!" Jake yelled.

The distraction gave Daniel enough time to sit up and throw his own punch at Jake.

Jake fell backward.

Mitch rushed in.

"Daniel! Look out!" Cassie shouted, pulling her arms against the zip ties, trying to get free.

Mitch ran straight at Daniel but merely shoved him aside and ran out the door.

"Mitch!" Jake jumped to his feet, rubbing his jaw. "Get back here!"

Cassie leaned forward, the chair fastened to her arms and legs. Then she wrenched her body up and stood with as much force as she could muster. The zip ties around her ankles snapped, and she fell back to a seated position.

Daniel stood ready, facing Jake with his fists raised.

Jake glanced at Cassie's free ankles and back at Daniel. He bolted for the door and ran down the stairs after Mitch.

"Cassie!" Daniel rushed to her. "Are you okay?"

She managed to force a nod. "Call 911. Hurry!"

Daniel pulled out his phone and punched in the number. He ran to the window and looked down to the street. "Send someone quick! To Banford! We found Lloyd Hutchins's real murderers, and they tried kidnapping my friend." He pointed out the window. "They're heading east on the highway, out of town."

Cassie sat patiently while Daniel gave the operator a description of the truck and shared other details. Pumpkin chirped and rubbed against her leg.

After a minute, Daniel hit the speaker button on his phone. Music filled the room as he set the phone on the floor beside Cassie and looked at her wrists. "I'm on hold while she notifies the police." He gasped. "You're bleeding."

Cassie looked at the rough, red rings around her wrists beneath the zip ties. She was cut in a couple of different places, but only a little blood was present.

Daniel ran to a kitchen drawer and returned with a pair of scissors. He cut the knobs off the zip ties, and they fell to the floor.

Cassie sighed in relief and rubbed her wrists. They were chaffed and sore.

He knelt before her, carefully taking her hands in his own, and closely examined her wrists. "I think you'll be okay. The cuts don't look deep." He lifted his eyes and stared into hers.

Cassie gulped. His eyes were bluer than she'd ever seen them and filled with a genuine concern. "Thank you," she choked out.

"I'm just glad you're okay." He remained kneeling, holding her hands.

They stared at each other for a moment before Daniel lifted his hand and tucked a loose curl behind Cassie's ear. She threw her arms around his neck.

He stood and pulled her to her feet, wrapping her in a tight hug. He smelled like cinnamon, and it reminded her of Gramma Merrick's apple pie.

Cassie took a shaky breath and rested her forehead on his chest. He gently rubbed her back. She felt so safe in his arms, but she quickly told herself it was only because of the rescue.

"Sir?" The operator's voice cut off the music coming through the phone.

Daniel released the hug but held onto one of Cassie's hands as he stretched to the floor and grabbed his phone. He turned off the speaker and pressed the phone to his ear. "Yes, I'm here."

Cassie let go of his hand while he finished telling the operator their location and his own name and address, as the 911 caller. She picked Pumpkin up and cradled her in her arms. The cat purred loudly and settled into the hug.

"She saved you, you know. Not me." Daniel pocketed his phone. "When I came upstairs after locking up the store, she met me at the landing. I thought it was odd she was out there by herself, but when she led me to this apartment and scratched on the door, I knew something had to be wrong."

"You little darling!" Cassie nuzzled Pumpkin, who rubbed her face on Cassie's chin in response.

Daniel sat on a bar stool by the counter. "We're to wait here for Officer Welby. He's on his way."

"Well, that should be interesting." Cassie let Pumpkin down.

"Let's take care of those wrists and ankles in the meantime." Daniel took her hand and led her to the bathroom.

By the time Daniel helped Cassie tend her wounds and get cleaned up, Officer Welby finally arrived.

She showed him the laundry baskets and explained the whole situation—how she'd found the rope at the crime scene and figured out Lloyd must have stumbled upon someone's hidden fish cage.

Officer Welby scrawled notes in his notebook as she relayed how Bubba had shared with her the secret standings of the tournament.

Zach was first, because he happened to catch one of the escaped fish near the cage. Eric and Marjorie were second, but they legitimately caught a fish through the locks on the far end of the river. Third place belonged to Mitch and Jake—and the evidence of the fish cage lay in the apartment, before them.

Officer Welby examined the laundry baskets and made more notes.

Cassie told him the rest of the story—how Pumpkin snuck in going after the fishy smell of the baskets and everything that happened after Jake and Mitch caught her in the apartment.

The radio on Officer Welby's belt crackled. "Suspects apprehended at the roadblock east of Banford." He clicked the button on the device near his shoulder and tilted his head to talk into it. "Copy that. Evidence is clear the suspects were involved with the murder of Lloyd Hutchins. Bring them to lockup, and have Zach Brooks released from custody."

Cassie let out a little squeal and clapped her hands. Daniel grinned.

Officer Welby let go of the button and flipped the notebook shut. "Your friend should be free in time to catch the end of the barbecue tonight." He avoided looking at her.

"Thank you!" Cassie hopped up and down on the spot. "Are we free to go?"

He nodded and grabbed the laundry baskets. "You'll probably have a follow-up visit in a couple of days."

"Come on, Pumpkin!" Cassie called to her cat. "We need to call Anna!"

Chapter 25

"Here you go." Daniel handed Cassie a napkin, which she used to wipe ketchup from the edge of her paper plate.

They stood near the edge of the canal, overlooking the locks, with Anna and Lexy beside them. Country music blared from the speakers on the nearby bandstand.

"Thanks." She took another bite of her hot dog. While most of the barbecue attendees in the crowd preferred the hamburgers, hot dogs had remained her favourite since childhood.

"That was Zach." Anna hung up her phone. "He's on his way." Her smile stretched from ear to ear, and her eyes shone in the low sunlight.

"I'm so glad." Cassie gave her friend a side hug as she carefully balanced her plate with the other hand.

"It's too bad he can't claim first prize," Lexy whispered, so no one else nearby could hear.

"It's okay." Anna pressed her lips together. "He didn't have his teammate with him. And since it's almost certain the fish came from the cage anyway, he could never accept the prize money and feel right about it. Besides, it's probably better for Bubba's business if his own son doesn't take first prize." She giggled.

"True." Daniel nodded in agreement.

"Anyway, we'll be fine." Anna rubbed her belly. "I'm just happy we'll be together."

Lexy nearly spat out her hamburger. "Are you——?"

Anna's eyes widened as she realized her mistake. "Don't tell! I'm not supposed to tell yet!"

Lexy let out a small squeal and hugged her friend. "Congratulations!"

"Shh." Cassie put her finger to her mouth.

"Sorry." Lexy backed off and quieted down.

"Cassie! There you are!" Bubba wound his way through the crowd to get to her. "Thank you, darlin'!" He pulled her into a big, sweaty hug.

He reeked of fish.

This time, she didn't mind.

"I'm glad I could help."

"You come by the shop this week and pick yourself out a new set of binoculars." Bubba winked at her.

"Another set?" Daniel raised his eyebrows.

Cassie elbowed him. "Thanks, Bubba. But there's no need. You do a lot for me. We've used your boat like a thousand times."

"Oh!" Anna chimed in. "That reminds me! Doris and William came into the shop after you left."

"Who?" Lexy asked.

"From the bird club." Cassie nodded at Anna to continue.

"They boated by the nest site at dawn this morning. They saw a sparrow with a fledgling!"

"Oh!" Cassie clapped her hands together. "That's such great news!"

"What's a fledgling?" Daniel asked.

"A baby bird." Cassie tucked her hair behind her ear. "When birds leave their nest, they're pretty much the same size as adults already, but they have fuzzy little feathers sticking out for about another week or so until their full feathers fill in and they can fly."

"So, your endangered birds have successfully multiplied."

"Yes." She grinned. "I'm so excited!"

Anna gave her another side hug, holding her plate out in front. "Ew. You smell like fish." She stepped away and grinned.

"Bubba's hug." Cassie lifted her arm to her nose to smell her shirt sleeve.

"That reminds me," Daniel added. "You never told me why you smelled like skunk yesterday."

"Skunk?" Anna tilted her head at Cassie.

"You mean you didn't tell him about the pot?" Lexy giggled.

"Shush."

"Pot?" Daniel cocked an eyebrow. "This should be interesting."

"Thanks, Lex." Cassie gave her friend a crooked smile.

"Anytime!"

"All right, everyone!" The music cut out, and Bubba took the microphone on the bandstand and stood alongside the marina and car dealership owners. "Time to announce this year's winners."

The crowd whooped and hollered.

"You can tell me about the pot later." Daniel nudged Cassie, assuring her she wouldn't get away with keeping her story secret. He took her and the other girls' empty plates and walked to a nearby garbage can.

"But first, let's take a minute to acknowledge everything else that happened this weekend." Bubba held the microphone closer as he quieted his tone. "As we all know by now, the two scuzzballs who murdered Lloyd have been caught. And thanks to Cassie Bridgestone, my Zachy has been cleared of all charges and wrongdoing in the situation." He pointed across the crowd to Cassie. "Wave, Cassie."

Heat flooded her cheeks as the crowd turned to stare at her. She raised her arm in a small wave and quickly lowered it again.

"Cassie owns the Olde Crow store on the corner." Bubba pointed across the street toward her building. "Be sure to thank her by giving her your patronage."

The crowd clapped.

Cassie waved at Bubba, with her head tilted slightly downward. She hoped he'd move on to the next thing quickly.

"And now, let's—" Bubba stopped and stared ahead of him.

Zach squeezed his way through the crowd and appeared before the stage.

"C'mere, boy!" Bubba bellowed into the microphone.

Zach climbed the bandstand stairs and embraced his dad with a big hug. The crowd clapped and cheered again. Anna squealed and ran to Zach.

"All right!" Bubba wiped a tear from his eye and looked at the table on stage splayed out with prizes and trophies. "Let's give out some prizes!"

Bubba counted down from tenth place, handing the lucky winners their trophies, envelopes of money, and other prizes from his shop like fishing rods and tackle gift bags. When he announced a couple from the equestrian centre taking second place, Cassie knew Eric and Marjorie held their position in first with the biggest fish.

Sure enough, moments later Eric and Marjorie bounded up the bandstand stairs to collect their large trophy and super-sized cheque worth thirty thousand dollars. They stood with Bubba and the other sponsors for a few photos by the press and then ran to their prize truck and boat nearby for a few more. Eric climbed into the driver's seat and waved to the crowd.

"I guess they could use a new truck." Lexy scowled.

Cassie laughed. "True." Then she sighed. She had to make sure she apologized to them for her erratic behaviour earlier. No better time than the present, she figured. At least they'd be in a good mood now. Perhaps they'd actually be receptive to her apology.

"I'll be back in a bit."

The music started back up, and people began mingling again, making it easier to fish her way through the crowd toward Eric and Marjorie. People circled around them, admiring the truck and the boat. Cassie wondered if she should wait for another time, but she wanted to get it over with.

Eric stood with his hand grasping the side of his truck. He let out a loud laugh and with his other arm, gave the man he was talking with a friendly slap on the back. The man joined the laugh and then walked off. Eric leaned over to look in the truck bed.

"I bet you can fit a lot of fishing gear in there." Cassie stepped up beside him.

His smile faded. "What do you want?"

"I wanted to apologize," Cassie forced out the words. "To you and Marjorie—for my behaviour earlier today."

"What's that?" Marjorie came around from the other side of the truck.

"I'm sorry about how I treated you today. It was rude and uncalled for, and I shouldn't have done it."

"That's right, you shouldn't have." Marjorie nodded once to drive home her point.

"At least you found out who'd really gone and done it." Eric slapped her back, as he had the other man's. "Consider us even, then, for almost flippin' your boat." His wide grin revealed a missing tooth Cassie hadn't noticed before.

"Done."

Relieved to have that over with, Cassie headed back into the crowd and turned sideways to squeeze through a tight spot. Up ahead, a familiar grey bun caught her eye. Gladys Hutchins.

Cassie quickened her step to catch up to the woman and tapped her on the shoulder.

"Gladys. Hi!"

"Oh, it's you." Gladys turned, her purse dangling from her arm. She didn't look pleased to see Cassie, but at least she didn't make a run for it.

"Um, how's Judd?" Cassie dared to ask.

"Who's this, Mama?" A woman placed her hand on Gladys's arm.

"That doughnut woman." Gladys pursed her lips.

"Oh!" The woman extended her hand. "I'm Jenny, Gladys's daughter."

"From BC?" Cassie shook her hand.

"Yes."

"I'm Cassie. Sorry for your loss."

"Thank you." Jenny smiled. "And thank you for helping Judd."

Cassie furrowed her brows. Helping Judd? What did she mean? "I didn't—"

"If you hadn't stepped in," Jenny continued, "Judd could have gotten himself in a lot more trouble. As it stands, he hasn't sold anything yet, so the charges are less than what they could have been. You helped stop him from making a serious mistake."

"Oh." Cassie fiddled with the neckline of her shirt. "I see." She searched for something else to say. "Are you in town long?"

Jenny slipped her hand into the crook of her mother's arm. "Yes. I'll help Mama with the funeral arrangements and find a good place to live."

"I'm glad." Cassie smiled at Gladys.

Gladys gave a quick nod and tugged on Jenny's arm.

"Bye, Cassie." Jenny followed her mother's lead.

Cassie stood for a moment, pondering the unexpected conversation. Then headed back into the crowd.

"Got a sec?" Daniel met her halfway to Lexy and Anna. Anna was busy wrapped up in Zach's arms.

"I think Lexy might need rescuing." She pointed. Lexy sat by herself, with her legs dangling over the side of the canal, eating another hamburger.

Daniel turned around. "She'll be fine. Maggie's on her way over."

Sure enough, her brother, Rick, Maggie, and the kids, were weaving their way through the crowd toward Lexy.

Cassie relented and followed Daniel across the top of the lock gates. He was much more agile and confident this time. On the other side, he led her past the groups of people seated in various spots on the grass and farther down the path along the river until they were more alone.

He stopped at a quiet spot overlooking the water and grabbed her hand. She knew she should pull away, but she didn't want to. His touch sent shivers up and down her spine.

"You're an amazing woman, Cassie Bridgestone." Daniel turned her so he could look into her eyes.

He held both of her hands now, and the shivers in her

spine increased their tempo.

"Daniel—"

"Wait. Please." He gave her hands a gentle squeeze. "You've given me a lot to think about. I came to a small town, looking for a change, and for something to fill the void in my life. You've shown me that I need to work on me before I can enter a relationship."

"But, I—"

He squeezed her hands. "And I wanted to say you are one of the bravest, smartest, and craziest women I've ever met." He smiled at her. "And I look forward to building a friendship with you."

Her shoulders relaxed. "Thank you. I look forward to a friendship with you too."

Cassie was so glad Daniel had mentioned friendship. He really understood her heart's desires when it came to relationships and chose to respect her wishes. That meant a lot to her.

They turned and walked by the water in silence, and she took the time to thank God for the last few days.

Her future in Banford looked bright, and she couldn't wait to see what else God had in store for her.

DID YOU ENJOY THE BOOK?

It would make my heart sing if you'd leave an online REVIEW for *Fishers of Menace*. It's the best thing you can do for an author, next to buying the book. Thanks!

DO YOU WANT MORE?

Guess what? There's a SECRET VAULT with more about Banford! Sign up at wendyheuvel.com to become a member of the Tea With Wendy club. You'll also receive my newsletter.

You'll get access to:

❀ A DETAILED MAP OF BANFORD

❀ FLOOR PLANS OF CASSIE'S BUILDING
   (stores, apartments)

❀ AN EASTER EGG GUIDE

❀ PHOTOS

❀ PUZZLES & GAMES

❀ …and more!

Sign up at wendyheuvel.com to enter the SECRET VAULT.

COMING IN OCTOBER!

PRE-ORDER NOW!
wendyheuvel.com/books

ACKNOWLEDGEMENTS

When it came time to write these acknowledgements, I sat down with trepidation. So many people have helped shape who I am and in turn contributed to the writing of this book, that I could never possibly include everyone on two pages. I'd need a whole other book! So, I'll do the best I can in the space given.

First and foremost, my dearest husband. You have supported me in more ways than anyone can imagine. You've stood by me all these years, giving honest critiques, allowing me the time to write, and sending me to many courses and conferences – all counting on the fact that I would publish someday. And that day is here! I thank you for all the extra driving, cooking, cleaning, and working you've done during the stages of creating this book. I couldn't have completed any of this without your help. I love you.

Second, my kids. Thank you for putting up with my absence, sometimes days a time, where I'd hole up in my office to get my work done. I appreciate that you (mostly) respected my office time. Thank you for your support. Mama loves you!

And yes, I'm a crazy cat lady, so I'm going to thank my three kitties for keeping me company while I write. And my dear Cricket, who is the inspiration behind Pumpkin. I miss you. Also thanks to my monster dog, whose need for walks pulled me away from my desk to get fresh air every day.

Thank you to Moesjie, whose love of mysteries got me hooked on them as a child. Yes, you will get the first copy of *Fishers of Menace*. I'll make sure. Love you Mom! And Dad... it's been too many years since you've passed. You're the reason I love watching British mysteries, getting me hooked on them when I was a kid. I wish you were here to share this moment.

To Mom and Dad H, I love you! I thank you for your support, encouragement, and prayers.

To the Armorers: Thank you for sharpening me. Being in the group has brought me to a whole new level of writing ability. I look forward to growing with you even more in the future. And a special thanks to Kat and Tammera, who obliged my crazy timeline. You're the best!

Thank you to my launch team for being so supportive and working with me to launch this book. You guys rock!

Thank you, Kimberley, for your friendship, prayers, and last-minute proofing. You're beautiful and amazing.

Daniela, from Stunning Book Covers: I love your designs! Thank you for helping a newbie out while I figured out how to navigate the cover design process.

Laura and Lynn, from Red Adept Editing. You're both so skilled and I look forward to our future relationship.

Ruth Soukup, Jim Rubart, and Thomas Umstattd Jr. – your courses are amazing. I've learned so much from all of you, and I appreciate the personal touch you offer your students. I will recommend your courses forever and ever!

Thank you, Scott and Becky for the amazing work you do at Realm Makers. The connections I've made, the classes I've taken, the retreat, the conferences – all of it – incredible. Though this book is a cozy mystery, I'm forever a Realmie!

To the readers – you guys are awesome! Thank you for reading my book. I've been waiting years to be able to say that. Thanks for making my dream come true!

And thank you to my precious Father in heaven. Thank you for meeting with me every day, listening to my prayers, reminding me that You're always with me, and giving me the strength and courage to step forth and serve you through writing. May you always receive glory in everything I do.

ABOUT THE AUTHOR

WENDY HEUVEL solved the Rubik's Cube when she was eight, but now can't remember why she went into the next room. Canadian by birth, Dutch by blood, and British by heart, she resides on 26 acres with her husband, kids (Things 1, 2, 3, &4), three floofy kitties, and monster dog. She's passionate about Christian mission work, travelling, birding, and eating potatoes.

Sign up for *Tea with Wendy* newsletter for freebies, book news, access to the secret vault, special gifts and promotions:
https://www.wendyheuvel.com

FOLLOW WENDY:

f wendyheuvelauthor

⊙ @wendyheuvelauthor

P wendyheuvelauthor

🌐 wendyheuvel.com